RADIO SILENCE

CONNECT WITH ME

EMAIL >> ervinkeisha@yahoo.com

TWITTER >> www.twitter.com/keishaervin

FACEBOOK >> www.facebook.com/keisha.ervin

INSTAGRAM >> @keishaervin

SNAPCHAT >> kyrese99

YOUTUBE >> www.youtube.com/ColorMePynk

DEDICATION

When I wrote Chyna Black in 2005, I never thought I would end up here. So much has happened to me since then. I have experienced my fair share of ups, downs, heartbreak, lies and abuse. Back then I was this wide-eyed, naive, 23-year-old girl hungry for love. I didn't know my power or my worth. I thought that love meant putting up with someone's behavior no matter how much it made me feel bad. I was a ride or die chick. The only problem was that the man I was in love with wasn't riding for me and I was killing myself.

I put up with so much crap just because I didn't want to be alone. Being alone was the equivalent of dying to me. During my twenties, I kept on dating the same type of man over and over again. I didn't realize that I was going to keep attracting the same man until I learned my lesson. God will continue to test you until you've passed the test. Once you get to the point where you know what you will and won't put up with, you aren't thirsty for a relationship;

you love yourself so much, can't nobody play you and you know God got your back; the man of your dreams will appear.

Once I reached my thirties, all of this became clear. I had to get in a relationship with me first. I am the happiest I have ever been in my life. I found myself when I took the time to get to know me. Until you truly know yourself, anybody will be able to get over on you. So do the work, ladies. Don't let negative bullshit distract you from your destiny. Don't block your blessings. Love yourself the way that God loves you.

So grab a glass of wine, your favorite snack and snuggle up. You're about to go on the ride of your life. I pray that you all enjoy Radio Silence. Hit me up on any of my social media accounts when you're done and let me know what you think. And remember to expect the unexpected!!!

XOXO,
Keisha

"YOU GOT ME OUT HERE LOOKIN' THIRSTY." – ELLE MAI,
"I WISH"

CHAPTER ONE

<u>\<Messages   Carlos   Details</u>

So u really ain't gon' call and tell me happy birthday?

       Chyna's mama always told her never to love a nigga more than he loved her but there she was at her 34th birthday party eyeing the text message wondering should she press send. It was almost midnight and she hadn't heard from Carlos all day. She thought he would've at least reached out and wished her well on her special day but he hadn't and she was genuinely hurt. This wasn't how she envisioned her 34th birthday.

       It made no sense that she was dressed to the nines, drunk off Rosé and in her feelings. She thought that getting a table at her favorite club, Mandarin, and ordering numerous bottles of Armand de Brignac Brut Rosé would keep her mind off the hole in her heart. But instead, she sat on a white leather, tufted couch with a chilled glass of champagne in her black, stiletto-manicured hand wishing Carlos would feel some type of empathy for her.

From the moment they rekindled their romance earlier that spring, she'd envisioned that she'd be spending her birthday with him but there she sat feeling more alone than ever. Her friends, Asia, Brooke and Delicious, were enjoying her birthday more than she was. Her friends didn't know that she was suffering in silence. Chyna was good at masking her pain. She kept a smile on her face all the while her heart slowly shattered from Carlos' absence in her life. He needed to be there with her; so despite her better judgment, she pressed send.

She knew when she sobered up the next day she'd regret her actions but she was living in the moment and giving into her erratic emotions. Chyna took a sip from her glass and surveyed the crowd. Mandarin was packed and the vibe in the club was turnt. None of the other chicks in the spot had a thing on her. Everything from her Laura Govan inspired haircut to her ruby red lips was on point.

Chyna was serving 2015 Maleficent and loving it. She never left the house without being beat to the gods. She was always dressed to impress. Chyna had to keep up with the baby bitches that were coming up. She might've been in her 30's and considered old by younger chicks, but

Chyna was that bitch. She was drop dead gorgeous with or without makeup.

She stayed driving the dope boys crazy. Her round, doe-shaped eyes, chiseled cheekbones, deep dimples and full, sensuous lips made up her facial features. She had the kind of face that you became mesmerized by. Every feature was perfectly aligned. Hoes stayed mad at how pretty she was. Chyna stood at 5'3 and was considered slim/thick. Her breasts entered the room before she did. They were massive but like the IG model India Love, she carried them well.

For her birthday she rocked a black, sheer, lace, high neckline, long sleeve dress that hit the middle of her sumptuous thighs. A black bralette and a pair of high-waisted panties covered her tits and ass. On her feet was a sickening pair of Aquazzura black, strappy, suede and leather pumps.

Chyna stood up and placed her phone into the pocket of her dress. She had to rejoin the festivities before her friends became suspicious. They all thought she was over Carlos but Chyna couldn't erase her longing for him if she tried. He'd permanently cemented himself inside her soul. She was sure with time they'd find their way back to one another. *Once he get out of his feelings we'll be a'ight,* she tried to convince herself.

Drunk Chyna always made sense. She hated sober and rational Chyna. That bitch was annoying as hell. Chyna hated being a responsible adult. The fact that Carlos hadn't hit her up since he left her house a few weeks prior was killing her. She tried to be on some *fuck him* type shit. It actually worked for a few days but the heart wants what the heart wants and Chyna wanted Carlos badly. He'd touched parts of her that she didn't even know existed.

They'd had a whirlwind romance over the summer and she didn't want it to end. He'd become her drug of choice and she needed another hit before she spiraled out of control. Chyna rejoined her party and vibed out to Rihanna's *Bitch Better Have My Money.* She closed her eyes and swayed to the hard-hitting beat. The champagne and the weed she'd smoked before leaving the house had her on another level. You couldn't tell her she wasn't the baddest bitch in the world. Chyna felt invincible. She bent over and rolled her ass in a circle as her friends cheered her on.

"Aye-Aye-Aye!" Brooke threw her hands up in the air, amped.

She was happy to see her friend having a good time. Chyna deserved to be happy. She'd gone through hell and back. It was time to turn up and live life to the fullest. After poppin' her pussy Chyna stood up straight and cracked up laughing. Mandarin was lit and she was actually starting to have a good time. She was determined not to let her ailing heart win and ruin her night.

Mad dudes had been eye-fuckin' her all night. One in particular hadn't taken his eyes off of her since she walked through the door. Homeboy was FINE with a capital F. He could've easily been ex One Direction band member, Zayn Malik's, older brother. Loving to play hard to get, Chyna acted like she didn't notice him. She knew she had his full attention so she channeled her inner Beyoncé and swung her hips from side-to-side then dipped it down low.

She was in the best shape of her life and her choice of outfit showcased that. She felt like a queen. She just wished that Carlos was by her side confirming what she felt. She wanted nothing more than to kiss his soft lips and tell him how much she loved and missed him. It was beyond fucked up that on her birthday she was the only one without a boo. All of her friends were there with their significant others. Asia was with her husband Jaylen, Brooke was with her new boo Bobby and Delicious and Waymon were joined at the hip.

Chyna could've rung in her birthday with L.A. but she was good on fuckin' with him. Too much drama came along with them dating. He was Carlos' frenemy. She was over fuckin' with friends despite how bad she wanted to straddle L.A. and ride his dick until she came all over his long rod. Chyna could not continue to live her life on a whim and succumb to her often selfish desires. She had to think about other people and their feelings.

L.A. would be the one man that would remain off limits. Her heart belonged to Carlos anyway. She was unwilling to see past him. Exhausted from dancing and putting on a front for her friends as if she was happy, Chyna fanned her face with her hand. Her bladder was full of Rosé and she needed to pee.

"I'm about to go to the restroom. Watch my purse." She yelled in Asia's ear so she could hear over the loud music.

"Ok." Asia nodded.

Chyna walked through the crowd. All eyes were on her. She acted like she didn't see all of the stares coming her way. She had to concentrate on walking without falling. Six inch stilettos, alcohol and a slippery floor was a dangerous mix. Chyna felt like she was in the opening scene of the movie Belly as she walked slowly through the club. All of her senses were amplified. The dim, red lights seemed darker and the bass from the speakers vibrated like drums under her feet.

She was relieved when she made it to the restroom in one piece but was pissed to see the line to get into the restroom was backed up. Her feet were already hurting and she was seconds away from pissing on herself. Chyna got in line and leaned against the wall. She crossed her legs and clinched her pussy walls tight. Drunkenly, she pulled out her iPhone to see if Carlos had replied. To her surprise, she had one unread text message. Chyna's heart almost leapt out of her chest with excitement.

She quickly pressed the messages icon with hopes of seeing a reply from Carlos but the message wasn't from him. It was from L.A. Disappointment filled her core as she opened the message to see what he had to say.

<u><Messages   L.A.   Details</u>

Happy birthday, love. Now that ur 34 maybe you'll stop bullshittin' around & let a nigga get to know u. Hit me up when ur tired of being loyal to a nigga that ain't being loyal to u.

Chyna swallowed the huge lump that had formed in the center of her throat. L.A. had spoken the God's honest truth. She didn't owe Carlos shit yet here she was being faithful to a man that wasn't even hers. *How you gon' let a white boy have you dickmatized,* she asked herself. Unsure of how to respond to the message, she decided not to. Chyna didn't want to send L.A. mixed signals. Half the time she didn't know what she felt. Chyna barely knew if she was coming or going.

In dire need of a restroom stall, she dropped her arm down by her side and looked towards the restroom door in despair. The line hadn't moved an inch since she got in it. All of the women in line had become restless and angry. The girl at the head of the line had become fed up and begun banging on the door.

"Open the damn door!" The girl yelled, pounding her fist.

To everyone's dismay, whoever was inside didn't open up. The girl and another woman hit and kicked at the door together hoping that would work. Minutes later the door unlocked.

"Thank God." Chyna rolled her eyes and sighed.

As the line moved up she looked to see who had held the line up for so long. Chyna squinted her eyes at the girl. The chick looked oddly familiar but she couldn't place her face. She was a basic Betty with olive-colored skin, mousy brown hair and a Cindy Crawford mole above the corner of her lip. The girl reminded Chyna of any other Puerto Rican chick you'd find at a corner store bodega in the Bronx.

Where do I know her from, Chyna died to know as the girl hung her head low, embarrassingly and giggled. To everyone's surprise, she didn't come out of the restroom alone. A man was steps behind her. He was laughing as well as he zipped up his pants. They'd obviously just finished having a quickie. It was so dark and Chyna was so buzzed she couldn't make out the guy's face at first but as he neared, her nostrils flared. Chyna's chest tightened.

The guy was none other than Tyreik and the chick he was with was his wife! She'd be able to spot Tyreik anywhere. She studied his face half her life. His chocolate skin, menacing glare and buff physique haunted her dreams. Chyna wanted to look away but she couldn't take her eyes off of them as they strolled by. Loupita, Tyreik's wife, locked eyes with Chyna and immediately stopped laughing. She'd never forget the face of the woman who ruined the most special day of her life.

Loupita shot Chyna a look that could kill. Chyna arched her brow and looked her up-and-down as if to say *bitch please.* Then she focused in on Tyreik who was already staring at her. This was the second time she'd seen him in almost two years. He had the nerve to wrap his arms around his wife's waist and kiss the side of her face; all the while never breaking eye contact with Chyna.

Chyna wanted to take off her heels and chuck them at his head. *No this muthafucka don't call himself trying to make me jealous,* she thought as they disappeared into the crowd. Chyna was so mad she could spit. Tyreik had the audacity to try to be funny towards her when every piece of clothing on his back were items she'd bought. *The nerve of that muthafucka;* she folded her arms across her chest.

Completely sobered up, she finally made it to the front of the line. Chyna did her business and quickly made her way back to her table. She couldn't wait to spill the tea to her friends. Brooke and Asia would for sure wanna jump his lousy-ass. Before she could get back she was stopped by the fine Zayn look-a-like who'd been checking her out.

Chyna's clit instantly began to twitch. Homeboy was sexy as fuck. He was even cuter up close. He wasn't black and he certainly wasn't white. The guy was of some persuasion that was exotic and sexy as hell. Dude was tall and slim just how she liked 'em. He had a low-cut with thick, bushy eyebrows, sleepy, brown eyes, broad nose, goatee and succulent lips. He was about 5'11 and could most definitely get it how he wanted it.

With all the confidence in the world, the guy took her by the hand and stepped into her personal space. Chyna looked up into his eyes and became lost.

"You are beautiful," she slipped up and confessed.

"Thank you." He shot her a sly grin. "So are you."

"I did not mean to say that," Chyna's face burned red.

She didn't wanna seem too pressed even though she was swooning on the inside. She hadn't seen a man this good looking since she met Carlos and L.A.

"What's your name?" The guy asked.

"Chyna... yours?"

"Asif."

"Nice to meet you, Asif," she smiled.

"I would love to take you out sometime. Can I give you my number?"

"Sure." Chyna pulled out her phone and unlocked her screen.

She was overjoyed when she saw she had one unread text message. A smile spread across her face as she saw Carlos' name at the top of her text list. She instantly forgot about ole boy and opened the message. Chyna damn near dropped her phone when she saw a picture of him lying sound asleep with his head rested on Bellamy's stomach. His arm was wrapped around her waist as she lie on her back in a pink, silk negligee. Bellamy stared directly into the camera with a devilish grin on her face. The picture was followed up with a text that read:

<u>\<Messages   Carlos   Details</u>

Hopefully now you'll get the picture. He doesn't want you. You were nothing but a rebound, bitch. So stop embarrassing yourself and back the fuck off!!!

Chyna had never felt so violated in her life. Everything around her went silent. It was as if she was the only person in the club. Her body overheated and she felt faint. This was not how her birthday was supposed to go.

She wanted desperately to clap back, but what honestly could she say? Bellamy had her tied up against the ropes.

"Chyna?" Asif tried to get her attention to no avail.

Chyna was stuck in a trance of devastation. No one besides her and Bellamy knew what had taken place but she still felt humiliated. She was too damn old to be made to feel this dumb. But Chyna couldn't even front, she'd brought all of this on herself. She shouldn't have texted Carlos in the first place. That didn't stop her from wanting what she couldn't have.

"Chyna? Chyna?" Asif shook her shoulder gently to get her attention.

Chyna came back to reality and blinked her eyes.

"Huh?" She looked at him bewildered.

"Are you ok?" He asked concerned.

"Yeah," she lied. "I think I just had too much to drink. Here." She handed him her phone, still dazed.

Asif saved his number then handed the phone back to her.

"Call my phone so I can get your number," he requested.

Chyna wearily did what she was asked as quickly as possible to get him out of her face. She had to get somewhere and sit down before she passed out.

"You enjoy the rest of your night, beautiful." He rubbed her arm seductively then walked away.

Chyna inhaled deeply and exhaled slowly. She swore she was gonna have a panic attack. Bellamy was making it abundantly clear that Carlos was hers. Chyna knew he was but what they had hadn't died in just a few weeks. He and Bellamy would never have what they shared. It was fucked up but no picture was going to stop her from loving and wanting him. Bellamy had one-up'd her and made her look like a fool but it was all good. Chyna would get her man back and get revenge.

"REALLY WISH IT WAS YOU THAT WAS BLOWIN' UP MY PHONE." - ELLE MAI, "I WISH"

CHAPTER TWO

Carefully, India tip-toed up the stairs leading to her mother's loft-style bedroom. It was mid-afternoon but by the pitch blackness inside her mom's room you would think it was still nightfall. There wasn't a trace of sunlight anywhere. India was going to rectify that immediately. Quietly, she placed the serving tray she held onto her mother's makeup table then headed over to the window. With force, she pulled the curtains back and let the sunlight shine through.

Rays of sunshine danced around the room. India made her way across her mother's bedroom and opened another set of curtains. As she headed back over to pick up the tray she heard the all too familiar sound of her mother groaning. Chyna hated to be woken up. India couldn't help but laugh. Sometimes she swore God had played a cruel joke and she was the mother and her mom was the child.

Outside of their looks, India and Chyna were complete opposites. Both of them were stunningly beautiful. India possessed her mother's wild, raven black, curly hair, light-colored skin and big, brown eyes. Other than that, they had little in common. Since as far back as she could remember, India had been her mother's rock and support system.

India was always there to lift her mother's spirits and help her navigate her life. She'd seen her mother go through hell and back. She had a front row seat of Chyna being a single mom, dealing with no good men, shady publishers, bounced royalty checks and internet trolls. At first it was weird having a mom that was in the public eye.

When India was younger, she used to hate when random people interrupted their mother/daughter time to ask for autographs and pictures. Now she'd gotten used to it and admired her mom. Chyna was her idol. There weren't many teen moms that beat the odds and made a success of their life. Not only was Chyna a best-selling author but a YouTube star and makeup artist. Chyna raised India with only the help of her parents and brother. India's dad was nowhere to be found.

She'd only seen a picture of him once and it was a mugshot. Last she and her mom heard, her dad, LP, was in jail after being busted for running a drug trafficking ring. As a little girl, India hated not having her father around. She often wondered if there was something wrong with her that he didn't want to be in her life. But as she grew older she witnessed with her very own eyes how her mother would reach out to her father so they could have a relationship.

Twice Chyna tried and each time he failed to meet her halfway. Now at the age of fifteen, India was over having a father-figure in her life. Her mom had done a damn good job at playing the role of mother and father. Yes, she had her pitfalls and faults but India loved her unconditionally. The hardest thing she had to witness was her mother be decimated by her ex, Tyreik.

He treated her mom like shit. India hated seeing her mom give him her all only to get nothing in return but heartache. India vowed to never let a man do her that way. The day of the accident was like a gift and a curse. It was fucked up that Tyreik got hurt but it was a blessing that after that day he was out of their life for good.

Her mom seemed stronger than ever. She hadn't had a steady boyfriend since and India was fine with that. She had her mom back. The fun-loving, optimistic, goal-oriented mom she'd grown up with was back. The house was filled with joy once again. Sure, every now and then India had to play nurse to her mom, but it was ok.

It was August 22nd, the day after Chyna's birthday party. India knew for sure her mom would be hungover. Every year for her birthday she turned up. Being the good daughter she was, India had all of the hangover remedies her mother would need. Chyna screwed up her face and blocked the sun from her eyes with her hand. Her head was throbbing to the point that she thought it was going to explode.

"I'm melting. No sunlight," she groaned, sitting up.

Chyna was shocked to see that she was still dressed in her outfit from the night before. She'd slept so hard that she'd poked several holes in the lace of her dress.

"Well, this dress is ruined," she scoffed, feeling woozy.

"Here," India sat on the edge of her bed.

She carefully placed the serving tray over her mom's lap. Before Chyna was a glass of water, orange juice, two aspirins and a bowl of fruit that consisted of mangos, strawberries and grapes.

"Thank you, honey." Chyna popped the aspirin in her crusty, dry mouth and downed them with the glass of water.

The glass of water felt like heaven sliding down her throat. She needed the nourishment desperately.

"Oh my God, Ma, you look a mess." India laughed. "How much did you drink last night?"

"Chile," Chyna exhaled. "I stopped counting after bottle number three." She massaged her temples.

"Judging by the smeared mascara and the missing lash, you had fun."

"We kicked it." Chyna scratched the back of her head.

"I can smell the champagne oozing from your pores." India fanned her nose. "I don't see how you drink that stuff. Alcohol is disgusting. It literally tastes like rubbing alcohol."

"What the hell you mean alcohol is disgusting?" Chyna shrieked. "Who the hell you been drinking with? India, don't make me kick yo' ass all over this room." She questioned about to flip.

"Mom, calm down," India cracked up laughing. "Paw-Paw let me have a sip of champagne on New Year's Eve and it was terrible."

"Oh, I was getting ready to say." Chyna exhaled and chilled out.

"Trust me, you do not have to worry about me drinking or smoking. I plan on living until I'm 150. Alcohol and drugs will hinder that."

"Good girl. Don't be like me. Be better than me. Learn from my mistakes and don't repeat them." Chyna warned before laying back down.

Worrying about India was the least of her worries. India was a good girl in every sense of the word. She'd raised her right. Unlike Chyna when she was fifteen, India was fully focused on school. She wasn't even into boys yet. India loved playing her video games and getting good grades. She knew she was beautiful but didn't use her looks as a weapon like Chyna did.

She had her head on straight and was focused on her goals. She wanted to be a video game creator and planned on going to school for it. Chyna had complete confidence in India's future. She just had to get her own shit together. She had to get her mind off of dick and on her career.

It was time for Chyna to shake things up and make some big moves. But first she had to get through dealing with the hangover that was kicking her ass. She never would've gotten so drunk if she hadn't seen Tyreik and his wife or been verbally bitch-slapped by Bellamy. Her hangover was all their fault. Dealing with both catastrophes in one night was too much for anybody to handle.

Chyna loathed Tyreik but she hated Bellamy with a passion. The bitch had been trying her since the day they met. It sucked that she had Carlos and was constantly one-upping Chyna. It was like she was Chyna's middle-aged bully. Chyna wasn't used to this kind of torment. She didn't get bullied. She usually did the bullying. But the fact that Bellamy was so threatened by her had to mean something. She knew that Chyna still had a special place in Carlos' heart. It was only a matter of time before she got her man back.

"Oh, here." India reached inside her back pocket. "I forgot to give you the mail." She handed it to her mom.

Chyna flipped through the mail which mainly consisted of bills and junk mail. One particular letter stuck out amongst the rest. It was a letter from the IRS but it wasn't addressed to her. It was addressed to Tyreik. Chyna knew it was illegal to open mail that wasn't addressed to her but she didn't give a shit. It was sent to her house so she was going to open it.

As she opened the envelope, suddenly her headache went away. Chyna was nosey as hell. Sitting up on her elbow, she peeled the envelope open. Inside there was a letter from the IRS warning Tyreik about non-payment of his federal taxes. They were threatening to place liens against anything he owned and take money out of any bank account he had opened. Chyna looked down at the estimate and damn near choked. The nigga owed the federal government $150,000.

"Ohhhhh my God," she said in disbelief. "Jesus, be a fence."

"What?" India died to know. "Mom, you ain't been paying your taxes?"

"Hell yeah, I pay my taxes. Yo' mama ain't no damn fool. Two things I don't play about and that's my taxes and my food. This was addressed to Tyreik."

"He owes the IRS $150,000?" India gasped.

"Yep."

"Dang, he going to jail ain't he?"

"Eventually; if he doesn't pay what he owes." Chyna shook her head and placed the letter back inside the envelope. "Here, throw this away."

"You're not going to give it to him?"

"Nope. As far as I'm concerned, ain't shit came here."

"Ma, you a mess," India laughed. "Why is his mail still coming here anyway?" She quizzed.

"Your guess is just as good as mine. Maybe he doesn't want his new bride to know just how much of a piece of shit he really is."

"I still can't believe he's married. I'm happy it's not to you," India let out a sigh of relief.

"I'm happy it's not to me either. Look at God. Won't he do it?" Chyna laughed, picking up her phone.

It was almost three o'clock in the afternoon and she hadn't checked her phone once. She had so many missed calls and text messages her head started to spin. People were still hitting her up to say happy birthday. Chyna hoped and prayed that one of the missed calls would've been from Carlos but none of them were. She wanted so badly to hear from him. It seemed as if he was done with her for good.

With each second, minute and hour that passed it was apparent that there would be no happy birthday message from him. Brooke and Asia had texted her, as well as the guy from the club. A smile instantly spread across her face. It wasn't Carlos but a text from Asif would do.

"Oh Lord," India rolled her eyes.

"What?" Chyna giggled, caught off guard by her reaction.

"I know that look. New boo alert."

"Maybe." Chyna held her phone close to her chest like a little schoolgirl.

"And on that note, it's time for me to go." India stood up.

"Thank you again, baby doll, for the care package. You're such a sweet girl. Mama loves you so much."

"Love you too." India raced down the stairs.

Once the coast was clear, Chyna read the text message from Asif with glee.

<Messages   Asif   Details

What's up? This Asif. Let me know when you're free so we can have dinner. What you like to eat?

Chyna replied back and said:

Hey, how are you? Maybe we can meet up next Friday. I'm not picky, so wherever you choose will be ok.

Minutes later, Asif responded with a text that said:

That works for me. See you then, beautiful.

Chyna looked up at the ceiling beaming from the inside out. Her night and morning might've been shitty but things were slowly turning around for the kid.

The dressing room at Neiman Marcus was poppin'. Chyna, Delicious, Asia and Brooke had the whole entire dressing room to themselves for a private fitting. The store assistants pulled looks for them from some of the hottest designers in the world. There were clothes, shoes and bags from Alice and Olivia, Marchesa, Givenchy and Akris Punto.

The sales girls knew their commissions were going to be extra fat so they were working hard to please them. The whole crew was ready to blow a couple of bands. Fall was nearing and they had to get their fall/winter looks together. Chyna wouldn't be caught dead in last season ensembles.

Tired from trying on frock after frock, Asia sat on one of the leather benches eating a complimentary cookie. Asia wasn't your typical beauty. Being mixed with Asian and African American ancestry gave her an exotic appeal. Asia had long, black hair that almost reached her butt, slanted eyes and full lips. She was petite but had a set of hips and ass that could compete with any IG model.

She loved that she and her friends were all uniquely different. Brooklyn aka Brooke was tall and statuesque. She rocked a short, blonde, buzz cut that framed her heart-shaped face perfectly. She was shaped just like Tracee Ellis Ross. Asia only got to see her friends a few times out of the year. She cherished each moment with them.

Buzzed off the complimentary glasses of champagne they'd been given, Chyna stepped out of the dressing room in a black and pink, Alexander McQueen, mock-neck, sheer, wave-dot dress. The dress was an ethereal renaissance inspired work of art. Chyna was in love with it. She never felt more beautiful. It would be a great dress to wear on her date with Asif.

"What you think?" She smiled, twirling around.

The dress made her feel so girly and pretty.

"Yassssss, I love it!" Asia snapped her finger repeatedly.

"You think I should wear this on my date with ole boy?"

"Nah, it's too cutesy. You need something with a hint of sex appeal," Broke chimed in.

"Besides, I look cuter in it." Delicious stepped out in the exact same dress and posed.

"Ok, Single White Female." Chyna looked him up-and-down with displeasure.

"Don't be mad, boo-boo." Delicious gagged, sticking out his tongue.

"You saw me pick out this dress first. You hag," Chyna fumed.

"Sue did and I had the girl pull it for me too. Stop having such exquisite taste and we won't have this problem."

"I can't stand you." Chyna mean-mugged him.

She was secretly jealous because Delicious low-key did look better in the dress than she did.

"That's a'ight. I got something else that's even doper than this. So keep the li'l funky dress." Chyna went back into the dressing room.

"Girl, Waymon gon' love me in this!" Delicious admired himself in the full-length mirror. "A bitch look like a bag of money!"

"Where is he, by the way?" Brooke asked.

"On an audition. You know he's trying to be the next Michael B. Jordan."

"That's what's up. I hope he make it so he can give me the plug." Chyna said from behind the curtain.

"Girl, bye." Delicious waved her off. "Executive Producers stay in your inbox."

"Yeah, but ain't nobody offered me a job yet." Chyna slipped out of the dress. "I need to get my foot in the door so I can fuck some shit up and make an impact on the industry. I really feel like I have some great stories to tell."

"You will, girl. It just takes time," Asia assured.

"I mean, my Power recap videos really put me on the map but I don't wanna just do show recaps for YouTube. I wanna write for television and film. Y'all know my dream is to work with Felicia Abbot. Her show *The Girlfriend Experience* is like my favorite show ever. Her writing is phenomenal and let's not talk about how she's a black, female show runner which is practically unheard of in Hollywood. I hit her up on Twitter a week ago and told her who I was and that I'm dying to work with her. I doubt she responds but no harm in trying." Chyna slipped on her next outfit.

"I know she's seen your recap videos on the show. She's going to respond, watch."

"I hope so, friend." Chyna situated the dress then stepped out.

She was now wearing an orchid-colored, Cushnie et Ochs ribbed, one-shoulder, tie-front dress that hugged every inch of her frame. The dress showed just enough skin and screamed *come get it*. This was for sure the dress she was going to wear on her date.

"That's the one." Brooke said in awe.

"Yep, that'll get your pussy ate for sure," Delicious declared.

"First date goals, check!" Chyna high-fived him.

"I love it, friend," Asia nodded her head in approval. "How much does it cost?"

Chyna looked down at the price tag.

"Thirteen hundred."

"Ooh wee! Them royalty checks from Emotionally Unavailable must be good than a mug," Brooke joked.

"Y'all, it's doing so good and I wrote that book in a week and a half, had it edited and on sale a few days later. I have never written a book that fast in my life."

"Shit, you were writing about your life so it couldn't have been that hard to write," Asia said.

"Yeah, the writing process was easy as hell but dredging up all those fucked up memories about me and Tyreik's Ike and Tina relationship was painful as hell. I can't believe how stupid I was, y'all. Like, I straight caught myself crying for myself a few times while writing. I can't believe I allowed myself to be treated so bad. I never thought in a million years my child would ever witness the shit she did. She saw me emotionally and physically abused. I feel like such a shitty mom when I look back on all of that," Chyna confessed, sadly.

"That was your past, honey, and a part of your testimony. That book is gonna help and heal so many women. It's so many girls still going through that madness and they need to see that there is hope and that you can change your circumstances. Don't be crying for yourself. You need to be thanking God that you have been delivert!" Asia held Chyna by the wrist and shook her back-and-forth.

"I know that's right!" Chyna waved her hands in the air.

"My thing is, what do you think Tyreik is gonna say when he finds out about it?" Brooke questioned.

"I don't know and I really don't care. What he gon' do, whoop my ass? It's not like I lied about anything. It's my story and my truth. He can be mad all he wants. My book is the least of that nigga's worries. He owes the IRS $150,000."

"You say what now?" Delicious said in shock.

"Yes, ma'am. The letter came to the house the other day."

"Get the fuck outta here," Asia said in disbelief. "That nigga just wanna go to jail."

"Same thing I said," Chyna agreed.

"Hell naw. You gon' tell him the letter came?" Brooke asked.

"No! Fuck that nigga. I don't owe him shit. His mail shouldn't be coming to my house no way."

"Nah, Chyna, don't be like that. You need to tell him," Asia urged.

"Fuck that!" Brooke disagreed. "Chyna, you doing the right thing. It ain't yo' fault that muthafucka didn't get a change of address. Wit' his dumbass. I still can't believe you saw him in the club. I wish I would've been in line with you. I would've tripped his ass," she grimaced.

"Girl, I wanted to but I was so in shock I couldn't do nothing but stand there and stare. When I see him now it's like seeing a ghost." Chyna turned up her face as her phone rang.

She checked the screen to see who the caller was. It was L.A. Chyna inhaled deeply and wondered if she should answer. A part of her wanted to hear the sound of his voice and hear him talk that talk that only he could. L.A.'s swag was like no other. She loved how hip and thugged out he was.

Pushing her desires aside, she sent his call to voicemail. She'd made up her mind that she would not fuck with him. She was determined not to change her mind. L.A. was off limits even though deep down she wanted to fuck with him in the worst way.

No matter how much she lusted after him, Chyna knew she was no-good for him. She'd only end up hurting L.A. Her heart still ached daily for Carlos. No matter how hard she tried to push thoughts of him out of her brain, it was impossible. She had to move on from both men. Maybe Asif would do the trick? Maybe he would be the much needed distraction she needed to get over Carlos and push L.A. away for good?

"I KNOW YOU WANNA LOVE BUT I JUST WANNA

FUCK." – JACQUEES, "B.E.D."

CHAPTER THREE

For Chyna and Asif's first date she would be meeting him at a restaurant called Franco. Franco was a French restaurant that served French dishes with a modern twist. The restaurant had an extensive wine and beverage list that was committed to classic French cuisine. Ironically, Franco was located in the heart of Soulard where she lived.

Chyna had never heard of it. The reason why was because it was located inside the Soulard Market Apartment building. Upon entry, Chyna was thoroughly impressed. The restaurant was immaculate. Faux brick walls, industrial lighting, stone beams, sleek tables and a full wine bar made up the interior. Everything about Franco screamed five star.

Li'l daddy got good taste, Chyna thought. After being greeted by the hostess, she was escorted to her table where Asif awaited. Butterflies fluttered around in the pit of her stomach as she made her way over to him. She hadn't been on a first date in ages. Since her break up with

Tyreik, she was on her fuck niggas, get money shit. Chyna wasn't into the whole dating, let's get to know each other spiel.

She liked to fuck... hard and keep it moving. Catching feelings and revealing hopes and dreams wasn't her M.O. But there was something about Asif she wanted to explore. Chyna loved beautiful things. She gravitated towards things that piqued her interest and Asif had her nose wide open. The man was aesthetically pleasing. She couldn't wait to sit on his face.

A warm, inviting smile stretched across his face as Chyna inched closer. The look he was giving her let Chyna know that the Cushnie et Ochs dress she'd chosen was a winner. Asif didn't look too bad himself. He was on his grown man, uptown swag. He had a rugged sex appeal that was undeniable. The five o'clock shadow he donned gave him a smoldering bad boy flow.

His rebel without a cause outfit made him even more dangerous. He wore a black, leather, moto jacket, torn and tattered Lanvin white t-shirt that cost $395, black skinny jeans and tan, suede, Chelsea boots. Chyna noticed a slew of tattoos on his chest that she hadn't spotted the night they met. Tattoos were her weakness. *Oh we fuckin' tonight for sure,* she thought greeting him with a devilish grin.

"Damn, you look even more beautiful than I remember." Asif hugged her close and kissed her cheek.

"You ain't never lied," Chyna joked.

She knew he wasn't lying 'cause she knew she was killing it. Her hair was freshly cut, lined and styled. She wore a simple pair of diamond stud earrings and the Cartier Love Bracelets Carlos bought her. She knew that constantly wearing them were an unhealthy habit but she couldn't bear parting with them. A red, Alexander McQueen marabou, feather clutch and Bionda Castana fuchsia heels with delicate straps and lace-up ties adorned her pedicured feet.

"Let me get your chair for you." Asif pulled out her seat.

Chyna watched him in awe. She was honestly caught off guard by his chivalry. *What is this an episode of Downton Abbey,* she looked around for a camera crew. She wasn't used to a man being courteous and thoughtful. Chyna was used to fuckin' with dudes that thought Wing Stop was fine dining. Now-a-days, it was hard enough to get a man to open a door for you let alone pull out your chair.

"Where you come from?" She asked as he scooted her up to the table. "'Cause you can't be from St. Louis. They don't make niggas like you around here."

Asif sat opposite her and furrowed his brows.

"Aww fuck," Chyna said, noticing how uncomfortable he was. "My bad. I ain't mean to call you a nigga. Force of habit," she nervously giggled.

"But umm... what are you, by the way?"

"What am I?" Asif repeated, thrown off by her line of questioning.

"Yeah, like what persuasion are you 'cause you're obviously not black."

"My family is from Armenia. It's a small place that straddles Asia and Europe." Asif took a sip of his wine. "Does that answer your question?"

"For now." Chyna caught a hint of an attitude and threw it right back.

"I took the liberty of ordering you a 1975 Domaine Ramonet Montrachet Grand Cru Chardonnay. It's a really good year. Is that okay?"

"Oh you fancy, huh?" Chyna chuckled. "Sounds cool to me. I mean... I'm more of a Sutter Home Moscato kind of girl but this shit'll do." She took a swig then smacked her lips.

"Ooh... that hit you right in the back of the throat." Chyna closed one eye and tried her best not to cough.

"You're funny." Asif laughed, amused by her theatrics. "I've never met anyone like you."

"That's not the first time I've been told that. I'm not your average chick." Chyna sat back in her seat and crossed her legs.

"I see. I think that's what I like most about you."

"Don't get too attached, homeboy. After getting to know me you might change your mind. You'll soon learn that I'm very blunt, borderline rude; I'm not mushy and I don't do relationships."

"I'ma keep it 100 wit' you. I am looking for a relationship but it's gonna take a special kind of girl to fuck with me. I have a very... singular taste." Asif let his words linger in the air before taking another sip of his drink.

"Shit, you ain't scaring me. I'm down for whatever." Chyna said turned on by his lustful glare. "What you into, BDSM," she whispered. "I like that freaky shit. The last muthafucka I fucked wit' was on that. Tie me up and spank me. I'll play along."

"Nah," Asif grinned, shaking his head. "What I mean is I want someone I can take my time with. Get to know."

"Oh," Chyna replied, visibly disappointed.

I don't know if this is gon' work, she thought with a sigh. Asif was fine but he wasn't giving her the rough, aggressive behavior she was used to.

"So tell me about your family."

"Uhhhh," Chyna replied, already bored with the let's get to know each other portion of the date.

She wanted to fuck. It had been weeks since she last got her back cracked.

"I have a great relationship with my mother and father. I have an older brother and a half-sister who I don't talk to."

"Damn, really? Me and my twin sister are mad close."

"My best friends, Brooke and Asia, are like my sisters."

"That's what's up?" Asif nodded as the waitress came over to take their orders.

An hour and a half later, after dinner and small talk, the date was over. Chyna was all for walking home since the restaurant was right by her house but Asif insisted on driving her home and walking her to her door.

"I had a really great time," he said, as she placed her key into the lock.

"I did too." Chyna halfway told the truth.

The food was magnificent and the eye candy Asif was serving was superb but she would've gladly skipped the small talk and went straight to riding his cock. How did he not expect her to want to fuck him looking the way he did? That was all Chyna could think about the entire date. Visions of him sliding his dick into her pussy as she looked into his eyes flooded her brain.

Chyna had to have him. India was spending the night over a friend's house so she could invite him in and be as loud as she wanted. She was determined to get her way and have him in her king-sized bed.

"I would love to do this again sometime soon."

"How about," Chyna stepped closer and traced her index finger across his broad chest. "You do me right now." She bit into her lower lip seductively.

"You're something else. You know that?" Asif clenched his jaw.

He wanted to fuck Chyna bad but now wasn't the time. He was determined to get to know her better before taking it there.

"Come in." Chyna wrapped her arm around his neck and kissed him softly on the lips.

She could feel the hard-on inside his pants. It was obvious he wanted her just as bad as she wanted him. Asif inhaled deep and calmed himself down. It was taking everything inside of him not to give in to temptation. Chyna was one hell of a woman. He hadn't been able to take his eyes off the curves of her frame but it was time to say goodnight.

"Nah, I'ma head home but I'ma see you again soon, okay?" He assured with a kiss.

"Huuuuuh... okay." Chyna drew back and rolled her eyes.

She wasn't used to not getting her way.

"You're too pretty to be pouting; stop." Asif caressed her cheek.

"Whatever, you gon' give me that dick!" Chyna teased.

"Goodnight, Chyna." Asif laughed, heading towards his car.

"Goodnight my ass. We gon' fuck, nigga," she mumbled underneath her breath.

"THIS WHAT HAPPEN WHEN I THINK 'BOUT YOU." -

BRYSON TILLER, "EXCHANGE"

CHAPTER FOUR

"This what happen when I think 'bout you... I get in my feelings, yeah... I start reminiscing... Next time around I want it to be different," Chyna sang tenderly to herself as she lie on the floor with her earbuds in her ears.

Tears stung the brim of her eyes as she lay stalking Carlos' Instagram page. Looking at his pictures was the only way she felt connected and close to him. She hated to see the pics he posted of him and Bellamy all happily in love. No matter how much Chyna wanted to hate, she couldn't front; they looked perfect together. Visually, they were a stunning couple.

He seemed genuinely happy with her. Judging from his pics, he didn't miss Chyna at all. It fucked her up that he could move on as if what they shared over the summer wasn't life-changing. He was the only man that made her want to open up and love again. He made her want to be better. Carlos was the only dude she wanted to give her all to. All he had to do was give all of himself in exchange for accepting her apology and taking her back.

Chyna was unwilling to believe that he didn't think about her or wonder what she was doing or who she was fuckin'. He'd made it his business to lay claim on her pussy. He would for sure flip if he found out she was fuckin' somebody else, although she wasn't. Chyna would give anything to have that old thing back. He was her boo. The man she adored. It was fucked up to know that the man she adored, adored someone else.

Although she hated the bitch, she would gladly morph into Bellamy if that meant getting him back. She'd wear her skin, grow out her hair, dress like her, smile, master her mannerisms and personality if that would make him want her again. Chyna didn't know how she ended up in the position of wanting a man that obviously didn't want her. The only thing she knew for sure was that she could love Carlos far better than Bellamy ever could.

If given a third chance, she would never hurt him again. She would never spew words of hate when she got upset. She would prove herself to be trustworthy of his feelings. All Chyna needed was another chance to prove herself.

"Give me that damn phone!" Asia snatched Chyna's iPhone from out of her hand before she could stop her.

Chyna quickly jumped up but it was too late. Asia had already learned her dirty secret.

"Really, Chyna?" Asia sat down on the couch and shot her a look of disappointment.

"Don't judge me. I know it looks crazy but you don't understand." Chyna tried to explain.

"I understand that it's my last night in town and you're over here obsessing over this Jon B lookin' muthafucka."

"He does not look like Jon B," Chyna checked her.

"Whatever. You gotta let this shit go. It's over. He made his choice and now you have to deal with it. Stalking his Instagram page ain't gon' help you do that." Asia gave her phone back to her.

"I know." Chyna placed her head down, feeling guilty. "I just can't seem to shake this nigga. My heart straight feels like it has a fat chick sittin' on it. Every day it feels like I'm fallin' apart. Everywhere I go it seems like I see and hear his name. I wonder about him all the time. I love him, Asia, and I honestly don't know if that's ever gonna go away," she confessed.

"Love is one hell of drug." Brooke entered her plush sitting room with three glasses of wine in hand.

"Ain't it?" Chyna took her glass.

"That's why I don't fuck wit' it. That shit will have you lookin' dumb than a muthafucka. Kind of how Chyna lookin' right now," Brooke joked.

"Fuck you!" Chyna hit her with the middle finger. "I know I look stupid. I stand in my truth."

"For real." Brooke eased down on the floor and sat next to Chyna. "A woman in love is helpless like a dog. Her tongue is constantly hanging out, slobbering and shit. It's not a pretty sight. That's why I only love Hennessey, fried chicken and trap music."

"What happened on your date with ole boy? I was hoping he would take your mind off this infatuation you have with Carlos. 'Cause honestly, it's gettin' on my goddamn nerve." Asia sat back and drank her wine.

"It was cute," Chyna shrugged, unenthusiastically. "It's just something off about him. When I invited him in for a nightcap he said no. Like, who turns down good pussy? Especially, this good pussy? This some five star, grade A, presidential type pussy. I mean... how dare he disrespect this?" She ran her hand up-and-down her body.

"Bitch... every man don't wanna fuck right off the bat!" Asia looked at Chyna as if she were crazy. "Some men do like to find out your first and last name before sticking his dick in yo' ass."

"Now you know damn well I don't do anal," Chyna pursed her lips.

"Whatever, I ain't got time to play with you," Asia waved her off, fed up.

"I ain't used to a man not wanting to fuck me. He was all respectful and had manners and shit. I'm like, who raised you? What's wrong with you?"

"You sound so dumb," Asia said in sheer disbelief. "I swear you have the IQ of a Ritz cracker. Simmer that pussy of yours down. Take that muthafucka from a 10 and dial it down to a 2. Stop leading with your pussy and get to know the man. Hell, he might surprise you."

"Taking my time and getting to know a man is what got me over here stalking Carlos' Instagram page."

"Noooo... you didn't get to know Carlos; that's what got you fucked up. You got so caught up in the dick that you didn't ask all the necessary questions."

"You right," Chyna poked out her bottom lip.

"I personally say fuck Carlos and Asif," Brooke popped her lips. "I'm team L.A. all the way. That one right there keeps it real. You should be studying the ceiling of his bedroom and the gentle curve of his cock," she said with a laugh.

"You are such a freak," Asia shook her head.

"L.A. thinks he likes me but he don't like me for real," Chyna remarked, swallowing some wine.

"Oh, he likes you alright," Brooke countered.

"No, I'm not his type. He just doesn't know it yet. On some real shit, in a minute I'm about to be team Jesus and say fuck all these niggas. Men are too much of a headache and dating is way too evasive and stressful for a bitch like me. If I had Carlos back, I wouldn't have to worry about none of this shit."

"But you don't so see what's up with Asif and work on moving on," Asia encouraged.

Chyna heard her friends loud and clear but she still held out hope for a future with Carlos. No one would ever understand the stronghold he had on her heart. He'd worked his magic and captured her mind, heart and soul. No one would ever compete or be able to satisfy her needs like him.

She belonged with him. Chyna was firm on working her way back into his good graces. If she had the opportunity to see him face-to-face, she knew their flame would instantly be reignited. There was no way Carlos would be able to resist her charm.

"BOY, GET UP INSIDE IT. I WANT YOU TO HOMICIDE IT." – RIHANNA, "YEAH I SAID IT"

CHAPTER FIVE

Asif kept his promise and asked to see Chyna a week after their first date. Chyna really wasn't as energetic about date #2 but her mama always told her never turn down a free meal or a movie. Since then, they'd gone out several times. It's been a month since they started dating. That night, he invited her to his house for dinner. Instead of picking her up himself, Asif sent a car to get her.

Chyna would've liked it if he came to get her himself, but when she walked out of her apartment and saw a S-Class Maybach and Asif's personal chauffer waiting, she couldn't help but feel like Cinderella. *Asif sure know how to impress a bitch,* she thought as the chauffer held the door open for her. Chyna sat in the backseat and admired the cityscape as they made their way to his place.

The ride to his crib wasn't a long one. Asif stayed downtown in one of her favorite loft buildings. She'd ridden past the building several times and wondered what the lofts looked like inside. Now she'd finally get to see. The chauffer opened the door for her and escorted her into the building where a private elevator leading up to Asif's home awaited her.

"Shit, I feel like I'm in Fifty Shades of Grey for real." Chyna said to herself feeling a little bit overwhelmed.

Seconds later, the elevator reached the 5th floor and the doors slid open. Chyna instantly felt like she was transported into a loft in Tribeca, New York. Asif's crib was downtown luxury at its finest. Dude had a 3-story penthouse located in the highly sought-after Syndicate building. As soon as Chyna stepped inside she noticed the European-inspired kitchen with stainless GE appliances, California Closet additions to the kitchen in the form of pantries, a spacious living area, gas fireplace, top-of-the-line roller shades adorning every exterior window and hardwood floors. In the midst of all the glamour was Asif at his kitchen's stove preparing a sumptuous meal.

"A bitch could get used to this." Chyna looked around in awe.

Asif had Barry Manilow playing so he didn't hear her come in. He was in full Chef Boyardee mode. Despite his choice of music, Chyna thought he looked cute with his apron tied around his waist. Chyna tried to creep up behind him to surprise him but Asif ended up spotting her out of the corner of his eye.

"Damn, I didn't even hear you come in." He hurried and switched the music to something more urban and smooth.

He wiped his hands on a towel and greeted her with a warm hug. Chyna hugged him back and basked in his Clive Christian cologne. The scent was her favorite. She loved a man that smelled good. A great smelling cologne was an instant panty dropper.

"Ooh... shoes... you're gonna have to take them off," he said, abruptly. "I can't risk you scuffing up my floors."

Chyna looked down at her heels.

"But my heels are the focal point of my outfit," she argued.

Since they were dining in, she decided to be casually cute and rock a statement necklace, lightweight, floral print, bomber jacket, a black, oversized t-shirt, leather leggings and the popular, cobalt blue, Manolo Blahnik Hangisi satin, crystal-toe pumps that Carrie Bradshaw married Big in. If she removed her heels her whole look would be thrown off. She'd spent hours putting the ensemble together.

"There's a pair of brand new slippers by the elevator for you to put on."

"But these are Manolo Blahniks." Chyna turned up her face.

"I don't care," Asif laughed. "The slippers by the elevator are Chanel."

Chyna looked back reluctantly. *This is some bullshit,* she thought removing one heel at a time. She instantly morphed from a glamazon to a short tree stump in a matter of seconds.

"I want you to know I'm not happy about this," she groaned, placing her heels by the elevator door.

"You'll be alright. Besides, what I tell you about pouting? You're way too old and far too pretty for that." Asif resumed cooking.

Did this nigga just call me old, Chyna sat at the marble slab island and asked, "What you cooking? It smells good."

"Cajun shrimp and chicken pasta. I figured we'd have a light salad and bread to go with it."

"I'm down. A bitch like me hungry than a muthafucka."

Asif looked over his shoulder, not pleased with her choice of language.

"Oops, my bad. There I go again acting like a ghetto banshee. I assure you my mama raised me right."

"I believe you. Now act like it." Asif focused back on preparing their meal.

I'ma let that slide, Chyna held her tongue.

"So what do you do for a living 'cause this place is stunning." She looked up at the high ceilings.

"I'm the vice president of an ad agency."

"That sounds like a fun job."

"It is. I thoroughly enjoy my job. How does it feel to be a best-selling author?" Asif turned off the eye on the stove.

"I love it but what I really want to do is create stories for television and film. I've put a few feelers out there so we'll see what happens. Enough of that, though. What's up with the food? I'm hungry as fuck." Chyna rubbed her hands together like Birdman.

"Keep on talkin' reckless and I'ma put soap in your mouth." Asif warned with a laugh.

"I would prefer your penis but I digress," Chyna joked.

Asif's face turned beet red.

"I don't know if I'ma be able to handle you." He placed their plates down at the table to eat.

"You can't," she beamed with pride.

"Oh word? That's how you feel?"

"There hasn't been a man yet that could." Chyna took her seat at the dining room table.

"We'll see about that but umm... I wanted to ask you if you wanted to go with me next week to this bonfire my old high school is throwing. It's a yearly thing we do to catch up with one another."

"Yeah, I would love to meet your old classmates. I need to get the tea on you 'cause I know you aren't as squeaky clean as you seem."

"Oh trust, there's a darker side to me that I don't think even you could can handle."

"Mmm hmm." Chyna waved him off.

"Plus, my people gon' be there and I want you to meet them."

"We meeting families already?" Chyna raised her eyebrow, surprised.

"I gotta let them check you out so I can see if they're gonna be as crazy about you as I am."

"Look at you tryin' to talk all sweet so you can get the drawz. You ain't gotta do all that, boo-boo. You gon' get 'em anyway." Chyna winked her eye at him.

"Shut up, Chyna," Asif hung his head and laughed.

Over dinner and wine Chyna and Asif continued to get to know one another. Chyna decided to take Asia's advice and put her lustful urges to the side. She found it quite difficult being that Asif was so fuckin' handsome. Halfway through dinner, she found herself enjoying his conversation. Although he was the total opposite of her, she found him captivating. Asif was more on the conservative side but appreciated her raunchy, over-the-top humor.

He was a gracious host and an awesome cook. Chyna didn't mind spending more time with him without sex being involved. After the yummy meal he'd prepared, she was sure to keep coming around. Chyna's belly was full after two helpings of pasta and bread. She was not the girl to be shy to eat in front of a man. Homegirl liked to eat.

Once the table was cleared and the dishes were cleaned, she and Asif made their way over to the couch. All the lights were out. The light from the fireplace lit the room. Flickers of light from the flames bounced off the walls. It was the first day of October so the fireplace warmed up the expansive room. She and Asif sat on the couch, curled up, sipping an expensive bottle of wine she couldn't pronounce and vibed out to slow music. Before long, talking ceased and their bodies gravitated towards one another. Asif placed his lips upon hers and Chyna melted. All sense of decorum she had went out of the window.

Her body was on fire. It felt good to be touched by a man. Asif's hands roamed her face, neck, breasts and thighs. Chyna wanted to explode. His tongue was wreaking havoc on hers. He was a magnificent kisser. The way he made her feel was indescribable. She was high off his velvet kisses. She lie on her back with him on top of her. Her legs were fully spread apart.

She was ready and waiting for him to take her to the next level of pleasure. She was beyond ready to go to 3rd base. With each flicker of his tongue on her skin, she became more aroused. It seemed like they'd been on the couch making out for hours when Asif abruptly stood up. Chyna sat up on her elbows and gazed up at him hungrily. As soon as he gave the go ahead, she was going to devour him.

His dick was damn near bursting out of his jeans. The sight of it pressed against the fabric of his jeans damn near made her cum on herself. Asif looked down at Chyna. Her hard nipples poked through her bra. Her chest heaved up-and-down from being so aroused. Seeing her in such a primal state had his hormones on a thousand.

"I'll be right back." He announced before heading to the back.

"Awwwww shit! I'ma about to get some dick." Chyna sang pumping her fist in the air.

Unwilling to waste any time, she took off her clothes and lay fully naked on her side. *I'm about to fuck the shit outta this boy,* she cheesed, fully ready for the D. Chyna could hear his footsteps as he approached the living room. Her heart raced a mile a minute. This was the moment she'd been waiting for. They were finally going to bone. Asif returned to the living area and flicked on the light switch. *He like to fuck with the lights on,* Chyna thought shielding her eyes from the blinding lights.

"Chyna, what are you doing?" Asif asked flabbergasted.

Chyna removed her hand from over her eyes and found him standing there with his jacket and shoes on and his keys in his hand.

"What kind of kinky shit you into?" She asked confused. "Ohhhhhhhhh... I get it. So you wanna be on some old Driving Miss Daisy type shit. That's different but... I can get into it. I like role play." Chyna said, down for whatever.

"No, I'm about to take you home," he grinned, embarrassed for her.

"What?" Chyna sat up and covered her breasts, mortified. "You wasn't going to the back to get a rubber?"

"No." He died laughing.

"Oh my God. I feel like such an idiot." She rushed to put back on her clothes. "I thought after all that 5th grade clothes burning we just did we were about to fuck." She pulled her leather leggings up over her thighs.

"I told you I wanted to take my time with you." Asif walked up on her and caressed the side of her face.

He could see she was humiliated. He hadn't meant to lead her on.

"Chyna, baby... you're sexy as hell and you know that but you gotta chill with all the sex talk. Trust me, for a minute there I was thinkin' about saying fuck it and knocking you down but when I have sex with you I want you to be fully in tune with me. I'm not like all these other dudes out here. I like to get nasty and when it's time to go I don't stop. I wanna make sure you can handle that."

"Boy, bye. I been fuckin' since I was fifteen. Ain't shit you can throw at me I can't handle," she spat unimpressed by his speech.

"That's what your mouth say but we'll see. Now put your shoes on so I can take you home wit' your li'l hot ass."

"YOU GOT MY SOUL." – BRYSON TILLER,

"EXCHANGE"

CHAPTER SIX

Life for Carlos since his "break up" with Chyna had gone on as usual. His restaurant and tattoo shops were still highly successful. He had money coming in left and right. Every morning he smoked a blunt out on his balcony. Five days a week he exercised to relieve stress and on the weekends he rode his motorbike. Bellamy had moved in. Their old house that she got in the divorce settlement was now on the market.

He kinda liked her being there when he got home from a long day at work. She always had dinner prepared and a hot bath drawn for him. She was no longer his wife but Bellamy played the role of wife well. She knew how to please a man and keep him happy. She did everything a woman was supposed to do. She loved him despite his flaws, supported his dreams, fucked him in every positon imaginable, cooked and cleaned.

All of that was cool but that still didn't stop him from missing Chyna. He missed her like crazy. He tried to hide the fact that he was secretly regretting reconciling with Bellamy as well as he could. Each day that passed that task became increasingly difficult. That day, he'd just hopped out the shower and finished getting dressed.

Carlos searched high and low through his slew of shoeboxes for his favorite pair of black suede Tims when he came across a box filled with Polaroid pictures of him and Chyna. He'd completely forgotten about all the impromptu photo sessions they'd had while together. There were pictures of them on the landing the day he took her to see him ride his motorbike, them at the pool hugged up and a pic of her sitting between his legs on the hood of his Jeep while looking over the city.

He even found pics that he'd taken of her as she lay sound asleep next to him. Seeing the pics almost knocked Carlos off his feet. He'd done everything in his power to avoid seeing her face. He no longer went to the places he knew he'd run into her. He knew if he took one look into her big, brown eyes that he'd fall right back into her trap. He couldn't risk it but the fact was already proven as he stood mesmerized by a picture of her looking over her shoulder at him while smiling.

Carlos had damn near forgot just how striking she was. Her angelic face captured his heart every time he laid eyes on it. He missed everything about her. He missed having her in his bed. He missed her attitude, the way she walked, talked shit and her smooth, caramel skin.

He longed to hear her whimper his name in his ear as he stroked her middle. He loved Bellamy and always would. They'd grown up together but Chyna had his soul. The only problem was the two of them together equaled way too much drama. Both of them aimed to dominate. They were both two broken souls trying to find peace in one another.

But both of them were vindictive, defensive and explosive. They would never be able to make a relationship work. Too much had been said and done to try again. He would never forget or forgive her for the things she said about his son. When Chyna got mad, she went straight for the juggler and so did Carlos. They'd kill each other if they got back together.

Plus, he was never loyal if you let her tell it. He should've told her about Bellamy from the jump but he didn't wanna rock the boat until he was clear about his feelings for both women. At the time, he thought rekindling his relationship with Bellamy was the best thing to do for everyone. He had to see if the death of their son was the reason for their demise.

Now that they were a couple again, he realized that they're baby dying was only the icing on the cake of the shit show they called a marriage. The truth was that Carlos had changed and Bellamy hadn't. He was no longer the 17-year-old, impoverished, fixer-upper she fell in love with. He was a rich, successful man that longed to be challenged. Bellamy was way too accommodating and judgmental.

She did whatever he wanted her to. There wasn't any mystery there. With Chyna, he never knew what to expect. She always kept him on his toes. He loved her spunk and the fact that she was wild and carefree. He needed the spice she gave back in his life but he didn't want to hurt Bellamy twice. She was doing everything in her power to make their second go around successful. Carlos just wasn't into it. He wanted that old thing back. He wanted Chyna.

"Babe!" Bellamy called out from behind.

"Huh?" Carlos jumped and spun around with a guilty expression on his face.

Slyly, he held the picture of Chyna behind his back so Bellamy wouldn't see and glared at her. He might not have been in love with her anymore but he would never be able to deny her beauty. Bellamy was an Armenian goddess. Long, jet black curls draped past her shoulders. She had very intense, hazel eyes, a pencil thin nose and collagen-injected, pornstar lips.

A peach-colored, long sleeve, lace top and a pair of peach, high-waisted, form-fitting pants and nude Louboutin heels complimented her spray-tanned skin. Due to cosmetic surgery, Bellamy had tits and ass for days. Since high school, she'd been cute but plastic surgery took her to bad bitch status. Bellamy stayed shitting on hoes. She was a shark and one hell of a business woman. Her cutthroat work ethic was one of the things Carlos admired about her the most.

"What are you doing?" She eyed him suspiciously. "I've been calling your name for the last five minutes. You didn't hear me?"

"My fault. I was lookin' for my black Tims."

"They're right here." She reached up and pulled the box down from the shelf.

While her back was turned, Carlos stuffed the picture in his back pocket.

"I ain't even look up there." He shot her a nervous grin.

"Are you okay? You're acting weird." She eyed him quizzically.

"I'm good. Just hungry, that's all," he lied.

"Well hurry up and finish getting dressed. My brother is here and the food is starting to get cold."

"A'ight, here I come."

Once Bellamy was gone, Carlos let out a sigh of relief that he didn't get caught ogling over old pictures of his ex boo thang. Swiftly, he placed the Polaroid picture back inside the shoebox and buried the box under the hundreds of others he had. Carlos slipped on his boots and headed to the dining room. Bellamy and her twin brother, Asif, were at the table waiting for him. Bellamy had prepared a small feast of grilled asparagus, shrimp, salmon, steak, baked potatoes and salad.

"What's up, bro?" Asif greeted him with a hug.

"What up?" Carlos hugged him back. "How have you been? We haven't seen you in a while."

"Some broad got his nose wide open," Bellamy teased.

"Whatever, I'm good. As a matter-of-fact, I'm really good," Asif boyishly grinned.

"Yeah, he's been bouncing around the office smiling and giggling like he's a Disney princess." Bellamy placed Carlos' plate before him.

After fixing her own plate she immediately started to eat. Carlos hated when she ate without saying grace. It was so disrespectful to him. Carlos bowed his head and said grace alone before digging in.

"I've been dying to know what's got him so damn giddy," Bellamy continued.

"It's this chick I'm seeing. She's bad, man," Asif stated proudly. "Like, I'm starting to think she might be the one."

"Oh please." Bellamy waved him off. "You said that about the last one, then suddenly it was over and you never spoke of her again."

"Sis, I'm for real this time. This girl is different. I think she could really accept me for me."

"Oh word?" Carlos said happy for his brother-in-law.

"Yeah, I like her. She's a li'l rough around the edges but I'ma get her together."

"Baby, you want some wine?" Bellamy asked Carlos.

"Nah, I'ma drink water tonight. Now what you mean she's rough around the edges?" Carlos focused his attention back on Asif.

"She curses a lot, a li'l bit ghetto but in a good way and she's always tryin' to throw the pussy at me."

"What's wrong with that? Shit, she sounds like a good time to me," Carlos chuckled.

"She sounds disgusting," Bellamy griped. "Baby, would you like some shrimp?" She tried to put some on Carlos' plate.

"Nah, I'm good," he replied annoyed.

He wished that Bellamy would let him eat in peace and stop treating him like a baby.

"Look, bro, sex is a natural thing. If babygirl wanna fuck, she wanna fuck. Give her the D," Carlos urged.

"So you think it's appropriate for a woman to want to have sex with a man as soon as she meets him?" Bellamy quizzed.

"What's the point of waiting? We grown." Carlos shrugged his shoulders dismissively.

"Oh, I forgot. That's the shit you like. That's what she who will not be named did," Bellamy rolled her eyes, referring to Chyna.

"Chill," Carlos warned.

"I'm just sayin'—"

"Stop." Carlos cut her off.

"Mmm hmm," Bellamy sucked her teeth.

"Okay, this isn't about you two. This is about me," Asif jumped in.

"Tell us about shorty, man," Carlos urged.

"Every time we go out, she wanna smash but I keep telling her to chill. Like, the last time I seen her - we were at the crib, on the couch doing our thing and I get up to go take a leak and grab my keys so I can take her home; I come back and she's sprawled out on the couch butt naked. I mean, she had that monkey out!"

"What kind of sleazeball are you dealing with?" Bellamy wanted to throw up. "This girl sounds horrendous. Mommy and Daddy didn't raise you to date women like that. You need to find you a nice Armenian girl like me with morals," she smiled, brightly.

"She's a lot to handle but she's a sweet girl, though," Asif guaranteed.

"No, she's a whore," Bellamy spat.

"Let that man live. I like her, bro," Carlos gave Asif a pound.

"You would," Bellamy sneered.

"I like her too," Asif smiled, glowingly. "As a matter-of-fact, I want you both to meet her. I invited her to the bonfire."

"Don't introduce her to me 'cause I don't wanna meet her. Keep that slut-bucket away from me." Bellamy shot with an attitude.

"Sis, don't be like that. Promise me you'll be nice when you meet her," Asif pleaded.

"I'm not promising anything. I already don't like her. She's trash and you need to leave her ghetto-ass in the gutter."

"She'll be cool. I'll make sure she act right," Carlos promised.

"HARD TO MOVE ON WHEN YOU ALWAYS REGRET

ONE." - MIGUEL FEAT. J. COLE, "ALL I WANT IS YOU"

CHAPTER SEVEN

It was a cool 55 degrees outside as Asif and Chyna pulled up to the bonfire. Nightfall was fast approaching. Pink hues cascaded over the afternoon sky. Cars were lined up-and-down the street. People were heading towards the big park where the bonfire was being held with lawn chairs, blankets, food and drinks. Everyone was dressed pretty casual in sweatshirts and sneakers.

Chyna had never been to a bonfire before so she didn't know what the proper attire was. She wanted to make a good impression on Asif's family and friends. She didn't want to come off too over-the-top or thotty, so she decided on wearing a light gray, floral print, oversized, tie-up trench coat, a white, skintight tank top with no bra, skinny leg, light denim jeans and floral print, Manolo Blahnik, pointed-toe pumps.

Her hair was on point, as always, with a sickening side part and a soft flat iron. She rocked a sultry, brown smoky eye, black winged liner, Queen Bee lashes, blush and extra glossy, nude lip gloss. She should've known she was doing too much when Asif picked her up in an olive-colored hooded jacket, black, Adidas logo t-shirt, olive joggers, no socks and fresh, white, Stan Smith Adidas.

"Fuck my life." She winced as he helped her walk through the wet grass.

With each step she took, her heels sunk into the mud. Chyna literally wanted to kill herself.

"I should've told you to bring some tennis shoes." Asif said feeling sorry for her.

"Uh, you think?" Chyna spat sarcastically. "My heels are fuckin' ruined."

"I'll buy you another pair."

"You sure in the hell are," she fumed.

Everyone was looking at her like she was a dumb-ass. Chyna couldn't even blame them. People were on straight chill mode. Beers were being chugged, burgers and brats were barbecued. For Chyna, her first bonfire experience was a complete disaster. *Lord Jesus, be a fence,* she prayed.

"You want me to get you something to drink? Maybe that'll make you feel better," Asif suggested.

"Yes please, and let it be hard liquor." Chyna stood in one spot trying her best not to sink into the mud.

As she stood by herself she noticed several side-eyes from a few chicks. They were looking her up-and-down with distaste.

"I know! I'm overdressed!" She shouted annoyed by their stares.

Ready to go home, she folded her arms across her chest and rolled her eyes. This was not how she wanted things to go. She was pretty sure Asif's people would judge her too and think she was trying to do the most. *Whatever; if they don't like me, they don't like me. I don't fuck with family no way,* she reminded herself.

Chyna looked over at Asif. He was in line for drinks and nowhere near the front. Surveying the crowd, she people watched. Everyone, besides her, was having fun. Maybe because they were comfortably dressed. Music was being played, there were several bonfires roaring and a mechanical bull for people to ride. All of Asif's classmates were smiling, hugging and catching up.

Chyna hated being the odd man out. She wished she knew someone else there besides Asif so she could have someone to talk to. Then her wish came true. The face she'd longed to see for weeks suddenly appeared out of thin air. Chyna swore she stopped breathing. *This can't be happening,* she thought staring around frantically. She wanted to see Carlos but not this way.

Her heartbeat slowed as well as time. He was as gorgeous as she'd remembered. His black hair was swept to the back and tapered on the side. His almond-shaped, brown eyes, kissable lips, scruffy beard and strong jaw made her heart palpitate. The black, leather, Balmain motorcycle jacket, crème knit sweater, faded, black, fitted jeans and distressed, lace-up boots enhanced his bad boy image that she adored.

It took everything in Chyna not to run across the field and leap into his arms. It was as if he felt her spirit from across the way. Suddenly, his eyes landed on her. Tears filled Chyna's eyes. It was at that moment she realized just how deep her feelings for him really were. Carlos was her beginning and end. Fuck getting to know Asif. He would never make her feel the way Carlos did. All she wanted was him.

Carlos stared at Chyna with a look of shock and confusion written on his face. He was stunned to see her at his high school's bonfire. She didn't know anyone he went to school with besides L.A. *If she's here with him, I'ma kill her,* he fumed. L.A. wasn't anywhere to be found so she wasn't there with him.

Chyna stood across the way looking like an angel. Carlos tried to stop himself from walking towards her but his feet wouldn't stop moving in her direction. Nothing else in the world mattered except him and her. He'd completely disregarded that he was there with Bellamy. He didn't care. All he wanted was to be close to Chyna. By the distraught look on her face, she'd been miserable without him too. Maybe they could give their love another try?

Chyna stood up straight and placed her shoulders back as Carlos came near. The tears she'd tried to fight back won and slipped down her cheek. She hadn't planned on crying when she saw him but the heavy emotions she'd been carrying around couldn't be contained. Carlos didn't say a word. He glared down into her tear-filled eyes and regretted every second they'd spent apart. The connection they had was too strong to ignore.

"Stop cryin'." He wiped her tears away.

"I'm not. My eyeballs are sweatin'," Chyna joked with a laugh.

Carlos clocked her wrist and saw she still rocked the bracelets he'd bought her. That obviously meant something. She still loved him. Maybe there was hope for them? Carlos wanted to wrap her up in his embrace and whisper in her ear that everything would be okay but they were interrupted by Asif. Chyna quickly turned to the side and wiped her face. She couldn't let Asif know she'd been crying.

"You didn't tell me you know my brother-in-law." He tried handing her a cold beer.

Chyna whipped her head around and exclaimed, "Your brother-in-law?"

"Well, my ex brother-in-law. He used to be married to my twin sister, Bellamy. They weren't together for a while but now they're back together. It's hella weird and complicated." He tried to explain.

"And how do you two know each other?" Carlos questioned perplexed.

"This is the girl I was tellin' you about over dinner." Asif draped his arm around Chyna's neck and pulled her close.

Chyna watched as Carlos' jaw tightened. He was pissed and she was scared as hell. Chyna didn't know what she had done in her past life to deserve to be placed in this fucked up situation. She wanted to move Asif's arm from around her to create some distance but she was frozen stiff. She honestly didn't know what to do. All she knew was that Carlos was pissed. At any moment, he was sure to Hulk out and lose it on everyone.

"There you two are." Bellamy tried to catch her breath. "I've been looking all over for you two. Diana talked my ear off." She kissed Carlos on the cheek then turned her attention to her brother and his date.

When she realized the girl he was with was Chyna, Bellamy nearly shit a brick.

"What is she doing here and why do you have your arm wrapped around her?" She yanked her brother's arm and pulled him away from Chyna.

"Stop! What are you doing?" Asif yelled caught off guard by her possessive behavior.

"What do you mean, what am I doing? What are you doing? Why are you with her?" Bellamy pointed her finger.

"You know Chyna too? This is the girl I told you about. The one I wanted you to meet." Asif looked back-and-forth between his sister and his date.

"Oh heeeeeell nah!" Bellamy shook her head. "You are not dating this slut-bucket."

"You are like so obsessed with me." Chyna flipped her imaginary long hair to the side.

"Oh please. You are a non-muthafuckin' factor, bitch. Everybody in St. Louis has had you!" She eyed Chyna repulsed.

Chyna closed her eyes and turned her head to the side, stumped. *She tried it,* she thought completely disturbed. Chyna screwed up her face and glared at Bellamy.

"Have you lost your fuckin' mind? 'Cause you must be crazy coming at me like that."

"I'm not scared of you!" Bellamy threw her hand around.

"Don't put yo' hand up 'cause that could get you popped," Chyna warned.

"Who the fuck are you?" Bellamy scoffed. "Oh, I know." She thought for a second.

"A whore. My brother has told me all about you. I know all about how you keep trying to throw that wretched pussy of yours at him and he keeps telling you no. You would think you would be embarrassed if a man keeps turning you down but not you. You just keep on going like the Energizer Bunny. I don't blame you though, brother. I wouldn't want to fuck her either. Who knows what kind of diseases she has marinating in that stretched out vagina of hers," she snickered.

"That's enough." Carlos stepped in front of her.

"Nah." Chyna pushed him out of the way. "She wanna talk shit. Let her talk that talk. Keep going," she encouraged.

She wanted to hear what else Bellamy had to say.

"Oh, you want more?" Bellamy stepped up into her face. "Okay... you're a pathetic excuse of a woman. Carlos didn't want you so now you try going after my brother? Who does that? Uh, you, whore. Get a life. I thought I made it clear the night you texted him to back off but apparently your dumb-ass didn't catch the hint!"

"The night she texted me?" Carlos interjected confused.

Bellamy pursed her lips. She immediately knew she'd fucked up. Turning her attention to Carlos, she gave him her sad, puppy dog face.

"She texted you the night of her birthday and I replied," she confessed, poking out her bottom lip.

"What the fuck are you doing going through my phone?" Carlos barked.

"I just wanted her to leave us alone!" Bellamy whined.

"Wait a minute," Asif jumped in. "You're the girl Carlos was messing with while he and my sister were apart?" He asked Chyna.

"Yeah," she replied, confidently. "And I would advise you to get your sister in check before I end up fuckin' you and taking her so-called man. And don't act like I can't have him back, bitch. That's why you're so pressed by me, 'cause you know I can."

"Girl, bye; he don't want you!" Bellamy flicked her wrist.

"No, he don't want you." Chyna stood so close to her their lips almost touched. "I see why things didn't work out between you two. You're an insecure, frigid bitch that can't hold a baby."

Bellamy's mouth dropped open and damn near hit the ground. She hadn't expected Chyna to go there. Chyna knew when she let the words slip out her mouth it would shut Bellamy down and hurt Carlos in the process. She didn't mean to have him caught in the crossfire but this was war. He'd have to become a casualty.

"Bitch, I will kill you!" Bellamy tried to lunge at her but Carlos stopped her.

Before she knew it, he'd swept her off the ground and lifted her up in the air.

"That's enough!"

"Nah, let her go!" Chyna challenged as they grew a crowd.

She was ready to whoop Bellamy's ass.

"Chyna, shut up," Carlos warned.

"You shut up!" She shot back.

"You ain't have to go there! You know that was foul as fuck!"

"Oh, so I'm just supposed to stand here and be every bitch and whore in the book and not say nothing? She can say I got a wretched pussy but I can't say nothing?" Chyna's bottom lip trembled she was so mad. "I don't think so! You got me fucked up!"

"That's why I don't fuck wit' you now, 'cause of your mouth!" Carlos pointed his finger in her face like a gun.

"Okay, don't fuck with me." Chyna spat not giving a fuck.

"I'ma catch you, bitch!" Bellamy warned, flinging her arms in the air. "On my son, I'ma beat yo' ass!"

"Shut up before I fuck your mother!" Chyna shot back as Carlos carted her off.

"Did that really just happen?" Asif stood perplexed.

"I'm sorry. I didn't want any of that to happen but your sister be on one. She had it coming." Chyna tried to calm down but found it difficult.

"You okay?" Asif asked concerned.

"Yeah, I'm fine," she lied.

"You sure?" He asked again.

"Yeah."

"I'll be right back. Let me go check on my sister." Asif gently rubbed her shoulder before disappearing into the crowd.

Chyna paced back-and-forth unsure of what to do. Things between her and Carlos were more fucked up than ever. She had to stop throwing baby shots every time she got mad. It wasn't right on any level but what was she to do when her back was pinned up against the wall? Chyna wasn't a punk and she wasn't going to start being one today. She was so mad she could spit. She hadn't been tried like that by a bitch since high school. Bellamy would forever have an ass whooping on reserve. At that moment, Carlos could get it too.

"Fuck him and that bitch!" She said out loud to herself.

"What bitch?" She heard a familiar voice say.

Chyna looked up to find L.A. standing before her.

"What is this, Chyna run into all the niggas she fuck wit' day?" She threw her hands up, exasperated.

"Who made you mad? Who I need to fuck up?" He grinned taking a toke off a blunt.

"Let me see that." She held out her hand.

L.A. handed her the blunt and watched her take a long, deep pull. Homegirl was stressed the fuck out. Chyna inhaled the potent marijuana and exhaled it into the night air. She hadn't expected to run into L.A. but he was a welcome distraction from all of the madness. He towered over her with a silly, infectious grin on his face that trickled over to her. Out of nowhere, Chyna started cracking up laughing.

"What's so funny?" He asked loving to see her smile.

"Life is funny, my nigga." Chyna took another drag then handed him back the blunt.

"You cool now?" He questioned, concerned.

"Yeah, I'm cool." Chyna took a minute to drink him in.

L.A. looked good, really good. A Living Single, grey, distressed hat was cocked low over his bushy eyebrows and diamond-shaped eyes. His caramel skin, slim face, smooth beard and mouthwatering lips called her name. He was 6'3 and 180 pounds of honey goodness. He had a ripped, athletic build that would make any woman drool.

Like Carlos, his body was filled with tattoos. The nigga stayed on the wavy side of things. He always rocked the hottest labels and jewels. That night was no different. The fitted, denim, button-up, ripped jeans, gold Rolex watch and Gucci sneakers was lit. He had a New York swag about him that turned her on to the fullest.

"You been duckin' and dodging a nigga for weeks now. What's up?" He linked his pinky finger with hers.

Electricity shot through Chyna's veins. The attraction she had for L.A. was unparalleled. She'd been feeling him since the day they met but he was forbidden fruit. Chyna inhaled deeply because fuck if she didn't want to take a bite.

"We gotta get over this hump, ma. Until we get over this hump. It's just gon' be fucked up."

"I'm kinda seeing somebody right now." She stepped back, breaking their hand holding.

L.A. hung his head low and laughed. Chyna acted like her having a man was going to stop him from pursuing her. He wanted her and L.A. had every intention of getting her. Whether she knew or not, she was his for the taking.

"You gon' get enough of fuckin' wit' these lames, love. I keep tellin' you to give me a chance but you hardheaded. What you scared?"

"No," Chyna lied, trying to seem tough.

"Yes you are." L.A. invaded her personal space and got in her face. "I can see it in your eyes. You want me just how I want you."

The seat of Chyna's panties instantly became wet. She wanted L.A. in the worst way but the fear of falling madly in love with him and L.A. hurting her always took over.

"It's cool. Fuckin' wit' a nigga like me, I'd be scared too." He traced her bottom lip with his thumb.

"I am not scared of you." Chyna tried to make herself believe her own lies.

"You are. It's all good, though." He bent down and placed a soft kiss on the corner of her mouth. "I'ma wait on you."

"YOU AIN'T RIGHT." - JAZMINE SULLIVAN FEAT. MEEK MILL, "DUMB"

CHAPTER EIGHT

After the throw down at the bonfire, Chyna just knew that Asif would be turned off and want nothing more to do with her. She was so wrong. It was the total opposite. He seemed more turned on than ever by her. The whole car ride home he couldn't keep his hands off of her. He kept telling her that he never saw anyone stand up to his sister that way.

Chyna didn't know what to make of his sudden advances. Her head was still reeling from everything that happened. Nothing she ever said or did was right in Carlos' eyes. He would always hold onto their tumultuous past and deem her as the devil. Frankly, she was over him and his holier than thou attitude. He was the one that did her wrong. Not the other way around.

He should've been the one kissing her ass. If he didn't forgive her now, then he never would and she was starting to become okay with that. Especially after he took Bellamy's side after their fight and not hers. Wrong is wrong and Bellamy was dead wrong to come at her the way she did. Carlos needed to be happy Chyna said what she said instead of slapping the dog shit out of her like she wanted to. If she saw Carlos and Bellamy again it would be too soon.

Chyna was so in her own head that she didn't realize she was back at Asif's crib and they were walking through his door. Before she could protest and ask to be taken home, her coat was on the floor and he was pulling her tank top over her head. Asif scooped her up in his strong arms and carried her to his bedroom.

"Asif, wait a minute." Chyna tried to slow things down.

With the mood she was in, sex was the last thing on her mind.

"Shhhh, baby. It's time." He lay her down and took her nipple in his mouth.

Chyna loved to have her nipples sucked. Kissing her nipples was a direct line to her pussy. Asif was working magic on her breasts as he pulled off her jeans. Chyna wanted to press pause but his tongue had already landed on her clit.

"Fuck," she moaned as his hands gripped her thighs.

It was over after that. Chyna was aroused and ready to go. She knew damn well she had no business fucking Asif now that she knew he was Carlos' brother-in-law but fuck Carlos. He'd hurt her once again, so fuck his feelings. He obviously didn't give a fuck about hers. Asif placed on a condom and began blowing her back out. Chyna was there physically throughout the whole thing but mentally, she was still back at the bonfire.

It was crazy running into L.A. Seeing him actually calmed her down. He was the perfect antidote at the moment. Too bad they could never have a future together. Chyna tried to concentrate on what was happening but she'd mentally checked out. Asif was so into his performance that he didn't even notice her lack of enthusiasm. The only reason she was able to climax was because she envisioned Carlos' face the whole time. Asif came as well and lay by her side trying to catch his breath.

"That was good." He wiped sweat from his forehead. "Did you enjoy yourself as much as I did? I told you I was a beast." He bragged, pulling her close.

"Uh huh," she lied, ready to go.

All Chyna wanted to do was take a bath, curl up in bed with a pint of Edy's Double Fudge Brownie ice cream and watch a movie with her daughter. She'd had enough.

"Can I get a glass of water?" She asked pulling away from him.

"Yeah, the glasses are in the cabinet on the right," Asif instructed.

Mentally worn out and physically drained, Chyna climbed out of the bed and headed to the kitchen naked. Wearily, she found the cups and fixed herself a cold glass of ice water. The refreshing drink reenergized her a bit but it was still time for her to go home. She had to get in a quiet space and process the day.

With the glass of water in hand, she absent-mindedly sauntered back to the bedroom. When she returned, her eyes popped out of their sockets and she dropped the glass. The whole cup shattered around her bare feet but that was the least of her worries. The sight before her eyes was too much to bear. Asif sat in the middle of the bed, butt naked, on all fours with his butt tooted in the air towards her. A black, silicone, 5 inch dildo rested by his side.

"What the fuck are you doing?" Chyna screeched, sickened.

"It's my turn now." He wiggled his ass from side-to-side.

"No the fuck it ain't!"

"C'mon, Chyna, don't be like that. I thought you said you can handle anything? That you was down for whatever?"

"You really think I'm about to fuck you in the ass with that thing? You out yo' damn mind! You and yo' damn sister crazy! What the fuck happened to y'all in the womb? Did y'all mama not take her prenatal vitamins?" She jumped over the glass and grabbed her jeans and heels.

"Where you going?" Asif flipped over on his side.

"I'm gettin' the fuck up outta here!" Chyna ran to the living room.

"Nah, Chyna, come back!" Asif jumped out of the bed, hot on her tail.

"Uh ah, don't you come near me!" She held out her hand and stopped him dead in his tracks.

"But, Chyna—"

"Uh ah, nigga! Stand back! Stay yo' crazy-ass over there!" She warned.

"I should've known yo' ass was gay when I caught you listening to Barry Manilow," she hissed putting on her clothes. "Don't no damn straight man listen to no fuckin' Barry Manilow!"

"I'm not gay!"

"The hell you ain't!" Chyna looked at him like he was crazy. "The devil is a liar. Lord knows the one thing I hate more than drug store makeup is a liar. Nigga, you are gay!"

"I just like to have a li'l fun." Asif tried to explain.

"Baby, I'm all about fun but you take fun to a whole new level. Now when I leave here, don't you call me no mo', you understand?" She questioned holding the elevator door open.

"But, Chyna, I really like you. The way you went off on my sister was so empowering. It really turned me on."

"Sounds to me like you wanna fuck yo' sister! You need to gon' 'head and handle that, bruh! Now, don't call me ever again! Lose my goddamn number!" Chyna demanded as the elevator doors closed.

"YOU BITCHES GOT ME FUCKED UP." - CHRISS ZOE,

"CUT UP"

CHAPTER NINE

Eternal peace was all Chyna craved after the night she had. Seeing Carlos, arguing with Bellamy and learning that Asif liked his asshole plugged left her broken in half. Chyna didn't know how she was going to put herself back together again. She was really fucked up this time. When she got home that night, she drank a fifth of Jack while sitting alone in the dark.

She was so shaken up, whiskey was the only thing that could soothe her. After calling an emergency meeting with her friends for the following morning, she drank herself to sleep. The hangover she experienced when she woke made her regret every sip. Chyna could barely see straight. The headache that throbbed in her brain felt like someone was playing hockey with her temples.

She low-key wished she hadn't called the impromptu meeting because she'd overslept and was struggling to pull herself together. She had to give her friends the tea though. They had to know the hell she'd been through. Nowhere near in the mood to be cute, she threw on a pair of black, wafer shades, a black, Pretty Ratchet Thingz hoodie, leggings and Tims. She didn't even bother carrying a purse.

Chyna grabbed her iPhone, debit card, keys and was out the door. Even though it was partly cloudy outside, it was still far too bright for her sensitive eyes even with her shades on. Chyna propped her hoodie over her head and climbed into the back of the cab. Comfortably seated, she closed her eyes and tried to get some more shut eye but to her dismay, the cab pulled up to the restaurant faster than expected.

Beyond annoyed, Chyna paid the driver and groggily got out. She and the girls were meeting at Rooster. It was a fairly new restaurant located off of South Grand that specialized in crepes, sandwiches and brunch items. They also offered a unique selection of coffee, craft beer and the best Bloody Marys and Mimosas in town. A cool, warm breeze swept through the October air. It was 59 degrees. Brooke and Delicious were seated on the patio. Being outside was the last place Chyna wanted to be but she was almost an hour late so complaining wasn't an option.

"How you gon' call an emergency meeting and be an hour late?" Brooke side-eyed her.

"Yeah, we already ordered and started eating without you," Delicious added.

"That's fine. Eating is the last thing on my mind." Chyna sat at the table and slumped down in her seat.

"Uh oh, something really bad must've happened if her greedy-ass don't wanna eat," Brooke said worried.

"After I tell you about my night, you'll understand why I'm not hungry."

"You look terrible," Delicious eased back like she smelled.

"I feel terrible."

"I ordered you a Mimosa," Brooke announced.

"I don't want nothin' with alcohol in it." Chyna held her head. "I'm still drunk from last night."

"What the hell happened 'cause you called me at 1:00 in the morning like somebody died."

"Friend," Chyna eyed Brooke wearily. "Like, I'm still trying to process everything; it was so crazy."

"Oh, this shit about to be juicy." Delicious scooted his chair up to the table, ready for the tea.

"So I went to the bonfire with Asif. You know I told y'all he wanted me to meet his people. Well, we get there and I'm hella overdressed so everybody lookin' at me like I'm crazy. Everybody is in jogging pants and sweatshirts and shit. And here I am in a full-length trench and heels."

"Sounds sickening to me," Delicious snapped his finger in approval.

"It was a really cute outfit." Chyna grinned falling in love with her look all over again. "But nah fuck that, my floral print Manolo's got ruined from walking around in damp grass all night."

"Girl, noooooo!" Delicious clutched a pair of invisible pearls.

"You know I was pissed."

"That's fucked up. May they rest in peace." Delicious crossed his heart and threw it up to God. "Shit, that's enough; I don't even wanna hear no more." He shook his head.

"Nah, peep this." Chyna sat up and placed her elbows on the table. "Asif goes to get us some drinks so I'm standing by myself miserable as fuck. When I see—"

"Reese Witherspoon?" Delicious cut her off.

"No." Chyna shot him an evil glare.

"Ooh... Beyoncé?" Brooke quizzed, excited.

"No. Bitch, what?" Chyna screwed up her face. "Carlos! I saw Carlos!"

"Oh shit," Brooke waved her off, disappointed. "Girl, bye. We thought you was talkin' about somebody good."

"Girl, get yo' life. Anyway." Chyna resumed telling the story. "I'm like fucked up 'cause he was the last person I expected to see. I didn't know what the fuck was going on or what to do. He spots me and we're just staring at each other. He starts walking over to me and I damn near faint. Y'all," she looked back-and-forth between Brooke and Delicious.

"What, bitch?" Delicious said anxious.

"He looked so fuckin' good." Chyna bit into her bottom lip, turned on by the memory of him.

"Bitch, I ain't get out of bed this damn early in the morning for you to be masturbating over your ex boo in front of me." Delicious scowled.

"Yeah, tell the story before we get up and leave," Brooke frowned.

"Let me find out I'm hanging around a bunch of haters." Chyna rolled her eyes at both of them. "Okay, so we're face-to-face. We're lookin' at each other and I can tell by the way he was looking at me that he missed me too. Mind you, I'd completely forgotten about Asif. So this muthafucka comes back with our drinks and is like, 'so you know my brother-in-law'. And I'm like, you say what now?"

"His brother-in-law?" Delicious shrieked almost falling out of his chair.

"Yes, baby. Brother...in...law. Asif is Bellamy's twin brother!"

"Get the fuck outta here," Brooke said in disbelief.

"On my mama I ain't lying." Chyna placed her right hand up to God.

"That's crazy."

"Oh, but it gets worse," Chyna warned. "I'm trying to process the info I've just been given when Bellamy bitch-ass walks up."

"I can not stand that bitch!" Brooke balled up her fist and punched her hand. "I ain't never laid eyes on the ho but let me ever see her. I'm dragging her ass on sight."

"If I don't get to her first," Chyna declared. "As soon as she spots me, she starts talkin' hella reckless, y'all. Homegirl get to callin' me every bitch and whore in the book. Talkin' about I got a wretched, stretched out pussy and shit."

"No the fuck she didn't," Delicious gasped, appalled.

"Yes that Bangladesh lookin' bitch did." Chyna couldn't help but laugh.

"Oh, she gotta die. Where that ho live at?"

"Oh no, I handled it. I told that ho she was a frigid, insecure bitch that can't hold a baby."

Delicious and Brooke's eyes grew as wide as saucers.

"No you didn't, bitch!" Brooke held up her hand for a high-five.

"I sure in the fuck did." Chyna slapped her hand.

"I don't feel bad for the bitch. She deserves it," Delicious said not giving a fuck.

"That's crazy." Brooke's head began to spin.

"Oh, honey, I'm not done," Chyna stressed, amped as hell.

"There's more?" Delicious said in incredulity.

"Yes; so before we could bang, Carlos separates us and tells me I'm wrong for what I said and then me and him have words. Bellamy is going off about how she's gonna beat my ass and I'm like yeah-yeah, shut up before I fuck your mother." Chyna died laughing.

"You's a dirty bitch!" Delicious high-fived her, loving every minute.

"After all that, I'm ready to go home but somehow I end up at Asif's crib. Mind you, after I ethered his sister, this nigga is mad horny all of a sudden and wanna fuck. But I was by no means in the mood. He gets to kissing all on me and long story short... we end up fuckin'."

"You fucked him?" Delicious flushed in distress.

"Yeah."

"Was it worth the wait?" Brooke died to know.

"I don't remember any of it 'cause my mind just wasn't there. I was still tripping off everything that happened. So we get done smashing and I get up to go get a glass of water. I come back and, y'all," Chyna paused for dramatic flair.

"What? Tell us!" Delicious bounced up-and-down eagerly.

"I come back in the room and this nigga on the bed bustin' it wide open. He on all fours with a dildo beside him talkin' 'bout 'it's my turn now'."

"BITCH, YOU LYING!" Delicious slammed his fist down on the table and jumped out of his seat.

The other patrons turned and looked at him like he was crazy.

"I'm sorry." He apologized to everyone then retook his seat. "Chyna, are you for real?" He whispered.

"Yes! The nigga is gay."

"You sure, friend? Maybe you misunderstood. Maybe the dildo was for you," Brooke objected unwilling to believe the truth.

"Brooke, you sound like Asia right now. The nigga is gay! He's a cake boy. Asif is a disco-dancing, Oscar Wilde-reading, Streisand ticket-holding friend of Dorothy!" Chyna quoted her favorite movie, Clueless.

"You did think he was weird and the boy can dress." Brooke quickly came around. "Damn, he's really gay."

"Yes, gaaaaaay. Big gay," Chyna stressed still outdone.

"I can't believe that shit," Brooke giggled.

"Me either. But what I wanna know is why do I keep attracting the gay boys? I mean, do I look like a dude or something?"

"I mean, you are kinda broad in the shoulders," Delicious teased.

"Fuck you. I'm done with life." Chyna announced with gloom.

"Don't be like that." Delicious massaged her arm.

"Nah, for real, I am. I can't take no more bullshit. If one more fucked up thing happens to me, I'ma snap." She said as a text message came through on her phone.

Chyna eyed the screen unaware of the number.

"Who the fuck is texting me from a 636 number?" She opened the message only to learn it was from Tyreik.

"Really, God? Really? What the hell does he want?" Chyna's upper lip curled.

"Who?" Brooke leaned over to see who she was talking about.

"Tyreik. He's texting me sayin' we need to talk."

"About what?"

"That's what I'm trying to figure out." Chyna replied as she texted him back.

Seconds later, he responded.

"He says he would rather tell me in person instead of over the phone and asked can we meet in a few days."

"You gon' go?" Brooke arched her brow.

"I guess so," Chyna sighed. "Some more letters from the IRS came. I guess I'll go ahead and give it to him. I just hope he don't start no shit with me 'cause the way I'm feeling right now; anybody can get it."

"I'VE MOVED ON; OH I SWEAR I'VE MOVED ON."

— KEYON DIXON FEAT. SIR, "I'M GOOD" (BRYSON

TILLER, "DON'T" REMAKE)

CHAPTER TEN

Rain poured from the sky as Chyna placed on her heels. She was supposed to meet Tyreik at Soulard Coffee Garden twenty minutes prior but as always, Chyna was running late. She figured she'd make him wait since he'd made her wait almost two years to have a conversation with him. He could wait a few minutes for her. Besides, she was in no rush to see his face.

Tyreik had become a deathly ghost in her life, a figment of her imagination, a thorn in her side. She couldn't wait for him to be out of her life for good. She no longer wanted any ties to him. When they met she was going to get everything she'd been dying to say off of her chest and keep it pushing.

She was over the drama and longed for peace. She no longer wanted to be a part of the bullshit. Chyna wanted to focus on her career and her daughter. Men and dating only distracted and clouded her judgment. After the Asif debacle, she officially swore off all men. Chyna didn't want anything to do with the male species. If it wasn't about getting money and being drama free, she didn't want any parts of it.

Fully dressed and ready to go, she took one last look in the mirror. It was rainy and cold out so she rocked a dark gray, ribbed skull cap, gray, cashmere sweater, light gray, wool, trench coat, a gold Cartier watch, black jeans and black caged, pointed-toe booties. She was only going around the corner but she wouldn't dare meet Tyreik looking like a basic bitch.

She wouldn't be caught dead looking a mess in front of him. She would never let him catch her slipping. She had to make him see she was doing just fine without him. Chyna grabbed her umbrella and headed down the steps to India's room. India sat in front of her television with her Xbox Live headphones on, playing Warcraft with her online friends. She was such a tomboy and Chyna loved it. She would rather her be a tomboy than the hot in the ass teenager she was.

"India!" She got her attention.

"Ma'am." India took her headphones off.

"I'm about to head out for a minute."

"Where you going all dressed up?" India admired her mother's chic outfit.

"I'm going around the corner to the Coffee Garden to meet Tyreik."

"Why?" A look of dread washed over India's face.

"Oh, honey," Chyna rushed over to her daughter. "It's not what you think at all. Calm down. I'm only meeting with him to give him his mail," she assured holding India in her arms.

"You sure that's it?" India questioned skeptical.

She knew in the past her mother's major weakness was Tyreik. All he had to do was whisper a few sweet nothings in her ear and they'd be right back together.

"I promise; there is nothing else going on. Girl, Tyreik couldn't get back with me if he tried. I'm so cool on him."

"Okay." India decided to trust her mother's word.

"I won't be gone long. I'll be right back." Chyna kissed India on the forehead before leaving out.

Five minutes later, she pulled open the door to the Coffee Garden and stepped inside. Soulard Coffee Garden was one of Chyna's favorite restaurants. Their breakfast was off the chain. It was the place where she and Tyreik signed their lease together. Soulard Coffee Garden held so many memories for her. Chyna looked around and spotted him at a table in the back drinking a cup of coffee. *Since when this nigga start drinkin' coffee,* she thought.

Chyna closed her umbrella and stomped towards him like she was Naomi Campbell walking the runway at New York Fashion Week. As they locked eyes with one another, nothing but contempt and resentment ran through Chyna's veins. Tyreik seriously made her sick to her stomach now. He wasn't even as cute as she thought he was all those years.

It was funny how falling out of love with someone and removing the rose-colored glasses that shielded her eyes could reveal the truth. He looked like a big-ass ape. Trying not to throw up, Chyna slipped into the booth without speaking. There would be no pleasantries between them. He didn't deserve her kindness.

"What's up?" She looked past him with an attitude.

"Hi to you too, Chyna." Tyreik quipped, sarcastically.

"Say what you need to say, man."

"Look, I just called you here because I wanted to tell you to your face that I heard about yo' li'l book, Emotionally Unstable—"

"Don't play with me. You know damn well it's called Emotionally Unavailable." Chyna spat not in the mood for his childish games.

"Quite frankly, I don't give a fuck what it's called. I need for you to keep my name out of your mouth. I don't wanna be in none of yo' li'l delusional-ass, one-sided books. I'm a married man now. It's not my fault that I'm happy and you're not. I don't talk about you. Hell, I don't even think about you. I've moved on with my life so I suggest you stop with the bullshit and do the same."

"You finished or are you done?" Chyna cocked her head to the side unimpressed by his little rehearsed speech.

"I said all I have to say." Tyreik spat arrogantly.

"Okay, well let me say this." Chyna placed her elbows on the table and clasped her hands together. "I will write about whatever the fuck I want. Who gon' stop me? Not you." She rolled her neck.

"My lawyer will. So take the book down or I'm going to sue you for defamation of character," Tyreik warned.

"Boy, please," Chyna laughed. "Spell defamation of character."

Tyreik sat silent and scowled.

"That's what I thought. You can't even pay yo' damn taxes. How the fuck you gon' afford a lawyer to sue me?" She threw the letters from the IRS on the table.

Tyreik picked up the envelopes and saw that they had been opened.

"Who told you to open my mail?"

"I did! It came to my house so I opened it. It ain't my fault you too lazy and trifling to get a change of address," Chyna rolled her neck.

"See, that's why I stopped fuckin' wit' you. You always on that bullshit. It's always a problem wit' you. I ain't talked to yo' ass in almost two years and we right back where we left off - arguing!"

"Don't try to check me then and we'll be good. Check yo' wife, nigga. I ain't that bitch."

"Oh, that's why you mad?" Tyreik held his head back and laughed. "You mad 'cause she got the ring and you didn't?"

"Nigga, I don't want you," Chyna stressed, repulsed. "The Puerto Rican Princess can have yo' tired-ass. I already know what she got and trust me, it ain't no damn prize. To be honest wit' you, I low-key feel sorry for her. Babygirl is in for a world of trouble dealing with yo' lazy, mooching, lyin', abusive-ass. You ain't gon' do nothing but fuck up her life like you did mine."

"I fucked up yo' life or did you? Didn't nobody tell you to stay all those years. You knew what was up. You knew who the fuck I was when you got with me," Tyreik argued.

"You're right and I was dumb enough to think that I could change you but niggas like you don't change; you get worse. I thank God every day that I'm not with yo' ass no more. That accident was a blessing in disguise."

"You would think that me damn near dying was a blessing," Tyreik eyed her with hatred. "You are a fuckin' bitch."

"Thank you," Chyna shrugged her shoulders. "I'll take that."

"Man, fuck you. This conversation is going nowhere just like our relationship." Tyreik rose to his feet.

"That's the first thing you said this whole time that made some damn sense," Chyna agreed. "You big dummy."

"Just stay the fuck out my life," Tyreik advised, walking away.

"Not a problem, boo-boo! Keep your mail from coming to my house and we won't have no problems! You bum!" Chyna yelled over her shoulder.

Angry beyond belief, Chyna sat alone in the booth incensed. She was so sick of dealing with fuckboys. Tyreik was the king of them all. He was a cocky, son-of-a-bitch that didn't have a pot to piss in but had the nerve to treat her like she hadn't been his savior for years. *I practically raised that nigga,* she thought. *That muthafucka still ain't even paid me back for my damn TV.* Niggas were so quick to forget who'd been there for them when they were down and out.

He'd gotten with the Puerto Rican Princess and acted as if she was just a bitch off the street. Well, no more. Chyna was over being trampled over. She had to take her life back. Chyna grabbed her umbrella and stepped back outside into the dreadful pouring rain. It was raining even harder now. She hoped that Tyreik would be long gone by the time she left. Thank God there was no trace of him.

In a dark and gloomy mood, she began walking down 9th street. Rain slapped under the soles of her shoes as she slowly strolled home. Chyna walked slow because she was in no rush to get back. She rather enjoyed the rain. It always soothed her. Plus, she didn't want India to see her upset. She needed to get her attitude back in check before she walked through the door. As Chyna basked in the serenity of the rain, she could feel her phone vibrate against the side of her thigh.

She didn't feel like being bothered but checked her phone anyway. It might've been India calling. To her dismay, it was L.A.

"Lord, whhhhy?" She groaned, looking up at the sky.

Aggravated, Chyna sighed and answered the call.

"Hello?" She spoke with an attitude.

"Damn. Who pissed in your cereal?" L.A. joked, caught off guard by her brashness.

"I'm sorry." Chyna shook her head.

She was being a bitch to L.A. for no reason. She felt bad for being rude. L.A. wasn't the problem. She was.

"Hi, how are you?" She checked herself.

"I'm good. Just callin' to check on you. See what's up."

"Nonstop drama, that's what's been up." Chyna tried to shield herself from the brisk air.

"You wouldn't have any drama if you would stop bullshittin' and give a nigga like me a chance," L.A. said smoothly.

"L.A." Chyna stopped dead in her tracks. "I like you, I do. Lord knows, I would like nothing more than to sit on your penis but messing around with you would only add to my drama. I don't need that. I have gone through enough. I just want to concentrate on my daughter and my career. I don't want to be a pawn in this li'l sick game of chess you and Carlos have going on. I—"

"Hold up. Let me stop you right there." L.A. cut her off mid-sentence. "I ain't in competition with nobody. I want you... flat out. That shit you had with Los was some bullshit and you know it. He's with Bellamy. He made his choice—"

"And I'm making mine." Chyna stood her ground. "You and I can't be anything more than friends. I really hope you can understand that."

"I hear what you're saying but I'm not giving up on you. Chyna Black, you will be mine," he declared confidently.

"I'MA KEEP RUNNIN' 'CAUSE A WINNER DON'T QUIT

ON THEMSELVES." –BEYONCÉ FEAT. KENDRICK LAMAR,

"FREEDOM"

CHAPTER ELEVEN

Being constantly tried on a consistent basis had really done a number on Chyna. Her showdown with Tyreik was the absolute last straw. Chyna was done with everyone. She had to take some time to herself to get her mind right. She had to go radio silent. She had to find some inner peace before she self-destructed. During her moment of silence, she figured she must be the cause of her problems. No single person on earth had this much drama and not be the creator of it all.

She'd known she'd get a negative reaction about the book from Tyreik and didn't care. She knew that pining after Carlos would land her nowhere besides with a broken heart. Chyna knew fucking with Asif was a waste of time. She found him extremely attractive but the chemistry just wasn't there. She'd forced herself to try and build something with him to prove that she didn't need sex to make her feel whole.

Now here she was suffering the consequences of all of her actions. She thought at the age of 34 all her drama would've ended by now and she would've known better. But Chyna was just as clueless about life and love as she was when she was fifteen. She had to get it together and fast. Her sanity depended on it.

To her surprise, Chyna found that isolating herself from the outside world was the key to success. Not being distracted by men, sex and petty drama gave her the much needed time she needed to focus on what was really important. Chyna wanted to be a successful television and film writer. She wanted to be a producer, travel the world, lose ten more pounds, get married, buy a beach house in Malibu and make sure India was a well-educated, strong woman.

Everything she did in life was for India. She was the most important thing in her life. She was her best friend. The love of her life. Chyna truly enjoyed every waking moment they got to spend with one another. That Sunday she stood behind India flat ironing her hair. India had wild, curly hair for days. Chyna loved her daughter's luxurious, natural curls. She loved everything about India. If she never did anything right in life other than raise a phenomenal, well-adjusted, self-respecting, smart, loving child, she would be okay. India was by far her greatest creation and achievement ever.

"You got your clothes ready for school tomorrow?" She asked parting her hair into sections.

"Yeah." India winced.

She was beyond tender-headed. The girl acted like she was dying every time she got her hair combed.

"Oww, Mom, that hurts!" India yanked her head away.

"Girl, if you don't hold your head straight and stop acting like a baby." Chyna pulled her head back towards her. "I ain't getting ready to be doing your hair all night. I gotta film my Real Housewives of Atlanta review." She picked up the flat iron to straighten her hair when her iPhone beeped.

Someone had direct messaged her on Twitter. Chyna looked down at her phone which laid on the bathroom sink. Her heart almost leaped out of her chest. She'd received a message from Felicia Abbot.

"Oh my God!" She promptly put the flat iron down.

"What? Did you burn me?" India ducked her head down, nervously.

"No, girl! You would've felt it. India?!" Chyna shoved her phone into her face. "The executive producer of The Girlfriend Experience just direct messaged me. I hit her up over a month ago and she finally responded!"

"What did she say?" India said excited for her mom.

Chyna anxiously tapped on the message and read it.

"Holy shit! She said we should chat!" She jumped up-and-down with glee. "Oh my God! Thank you, Jesus!" She began to shout.

This was the opportunity she'd been waiting for. She'd prayed to God every night to open up a door for her. She knew she wasn't only meant to be a best-selling author. Chyna was destined to see her name in lights. She wanted to do it all. She wanted to write, produce, direct and act. She'd prayed that someone would see how talented she was and give her a shot to show what she could do. Her prayers were finally coming true.

"What are you going to say?" India watched as her mother freaked out.

"I'm gonna tell her hell yeah we can talk." Chyna stated bluntly.

"Mom, you can't curse."

"Well, I'm not going to say it like that," Chyna explained while typing.

She was so hype her fingers were shaking.

"Lord, thank you. Thank you, Jesus! Thank you!" She praised God and pressed send on her reply.

Two minutes passed and Felicia responded.

"She said, 'ok. I'll give you a shout this week. You're very talented and funny!'" Chyna shrieked, twirling around in a circle.

"Mom, that's so dope!" India cheered.

"India!" Chyna stopped twirling and looked at her. "This is what I've been waiting for. Do you know how this could change our lives if she offers me a job writing on her show? Oh my God! What if I can finally get to see my words on screen?!" Chyna began to cry.

"I've worked so hard to get to this point and to have someone like her take notice of me is crazy. I can't do nothing but thank God. I've always told you, India, where there is a will, there is a way. If you believe in God and work hard, he'll bless you with the desires of your heart."

"I know, Mom, and you deserve this. I'm so happy for you." India wrapped her arms around her mother's waist and hugged her tight.

"Thank you, baby." Chyna hugged her back. "Mama loves you so much." She kissed the top of her head. "Now, I gotta call everybody and tell them the good news!"

"But what about my hair?" India ran her hand across her head.

"Girl, I'll finish your hair later." Chyna flicked her wrist. "Mama's about to be a star!"

With Felicia's busy schedule, a few weeks went by before Chyna could pin down a meeting with her. For a minute, Chyna thought she was being given the run around again like so many times before by other Hollywood heavyweights. The entertainment industry was a very fickle, fake and shady business. Everyone wore a mask so she never knew who to really trust. After several disappointments, Chyna learned the hard way never to trust anything anyone had to say.

Agents and execs would hype her up and sell her a dream and she'd never hear from them again. If she wasn't being offered a contract, Chyna let shit go in one ear and out the other. But on that day, none of the past B.S. she'd been through mattered. The day she'd been praying for was finally here.

Chyna sat outside Felicia's office impatiently awaiting to be seen. She tried her best to keep her composure but on the inside she was freaking out. *I'm about to meet my idol,* she tapped her foot nervously. Chyna had been so blessed throughout her life. To go from being a high school dropout, teen mom on welfare to this was the thing dreams were made of. Moments like this didn't happen to girls like her.

Chyna was beyond grateful. Every day she thanked God. Suddenly it dawned on her that all of the turmoil she'd been going through lately was the devil trying to block her from her blessings. He knew she was about to be the shit. The devil knew she was on the cusp of greatness. Chyna realized that it wasn't until she got quiet that she was ready to receive what God had in store for her. There was no way Chyna was gonna fuck this up. She was sure she and Felicia would hit it off and she'd be hired and working in no time.

"Chyna Black," Felicia's receptionist got her attention. "Mrs. Abbot will see you now." The receptionist stood and led her to Felicia's office.

Chyna walked inside in awe. Felicia's office wasn't what she expected at all. It wasn't massive in size like she envisioned it to be. Is was a nice size office. There were faux brick walls, posters of all her hit shows, a black desk, an Apple computer, a red, leather couch, a coatrack with tons of dresses stored on it and tons of comic book memorabilia.

Felicia sat behind her desk finishing up a call. Visually, she was everything Chyna thought she would be. She'd seen her a million times in photos but to see her live in the flesh was a real treat. A smile a mile wide was stretched across her face. Chyna was awestruck by her girl next door features. Felicia was gorgeous. Her sun- kissed skin, round eyes, rosy cheeks and Julia Robert's smile lit up the room.

She wore a coral, matte lipstick that matched her coral and white, Donna Karen New York shift dress to perfection. The woman was the personification of a boss. The palms of Chyna's hands immediately started to sweat. *What have I gotten myself into?* She didn't know whether to sit, stand, curtsey or bow. Felicia could see the uncertainty on her face and gestured for her to have a seat. Chyna quickly did as she was told and placed her clutch in her lap. Seeing a black woman with so much power invigorated and terrified her all at the same time. *Blue Ivy, be a fence,* she prayed.

"Okay, son, I have to go now. I have someone waiting in my office," Felicia spoke into the phone. "Talk to you soon. Love you."

"We finally meet." She greeted Chyna with a smile.

"Yes, I'm so excited," Chyna beamed.

"You are one funny lady. Your recap videos of The Girlfriend Experience are hilarious. Me and The Writers' Room watch them all the time."

"Oh my God, to hear you say that is like mind-blowing to me." Chyna gushed with pride.

"So when you reached out to me you said you were an author."

"Yes." Chyna sat up straight. "I've been a published author since 2004."

"That's great. I did some research on you and you have quite a following. Your book reviews are great. Your audience really connects with you. Unfortunately, with my crazy schedule I haven't been able to read any of your work but I'm very impressed with what I've seen."

"Thank you so much. That really means a lot to me, coming from you. I've worked really hard to get where I'm at but writing for television is my dream."

"Do you have a spec of the show?" Felicia reached out her hand.

"A what? A what?" Chyna asked twice, caught off guard.

"A spec," Felicia repeated.

Chyna sat stumped.

"I'm sorry. I don't know what that is," she replied feeling dumb.

"A spec is when you create an episode of the show so I can see if you can adapt to my writing style and if you know how to write a dramedy," Felicia explained.

"I'm sorry. I don't have one." Chyna said feeling like a complete idiot and a failure.

A cold sweat washed over her. She'd royally screwed up.

"Well, you're gonna need one if you want to work for me. I must admit, Miss Black, that I'm very disappointed that you didn't come prepared," Felicia said sternly. "I expected so much more from you. You're a very talented girl but this business isn't just based off talent. You have to have skill as well."

It took every fiber of Chyna's being not to break down and cry. She'd blew it. She'd come this far and completely fucked everything up. If she didn't rectify the problem ASAP, she would probably never get another opportunity to work with Felicia again.

"I understand everything you're saying and please forgive me for not being prepared. To be honest with you, I came into this meeting thinking I had it all together but obviously I don't. What I can tell you, Mrs. Abbot—"

"Please, call me Felicia." She corrected her.

"Felicia," Chyna corrected herself. "I'm an extremely hard worker. Nothing has ever been handed to me. I've had to fight and work extra hard for everything that I've achieved. I've had a wonderful career as an author but television and film is where my heart is. I know that I have a lot to learn and I have no problem getting coffee, mopping the floors or running errands. Whatever I need to do in order to work with you and learn from you I will do. You've said in all of your interviews that you want to mentor young women so that they can have a chance to get to where you are. I'm that girl," Chyna stressed passionately.

"I'm willing to work my way up and while I'm working to prove to you just how bad I want this and how good of a writer I am, I'll be working on my spec. Just please... give me a chance to show you what I can do. I promise, I won't let you down," Chyna pleaded.

Felicia took a deep breath and let Chyna's words sink in.

"You know there will be a lot of long nights. If you don't have a solid home life or a solid relationship with your spouse things will fall apart," she gazed off somberly.

"This is a very stressful business. You'll be gone a lot. Your social life will become non-existent. You'll barley have time for your friends. I've been married for over 20 years and every day is a struggle to keep my marriage afloat. If you have children, you won't be as present in their lives as they'll need you to be. Thank God my son is grown now so I don't have to worry about that. But it was hard when he was younger. I missed all his school plays and sporting events. He resented me for years. Thankfully, he understands now all of the sacrifices I had to make. Are you ready for all of that? Are you sure this is what you really want?" Felicia eyed her quizzically.

"I want this more than the air I breathe," Chyna swore.

Felicia saw the hunger in her eyes. She liked it. Chyna reminded her a lot of herself when she was fresh in the business.

"Okay, I'll give you a shot. But it won't be in The Writers' Room. You'll be my assistant. Your first task is to attend the Entertainment Weekly party with me tonight. It starts at 7pm so I'll need you to contact my hairstylist, book me a nail appointment, make sure my makeup artist gets here on time, go to Saks and pick me out a dress, order car service and be there at the party to help me with anything else I may need. You got that?"

"I got it," Chyna cheesed really hard. "Thank you so much, Felicia. I swear you won't be disappointed."

"We'll see."

"WHEN I FIRST MET YA, YOU WAS FEELING ME BUT YOU DIDN'T TELL ME I HAD COMPETITION." – ELLE MAI, "I WISH"

CHAPTER TWELVE

Chyna never attended a party without looking like a ten. After spending her day running around for Felicia, she had no choice but to show up to the Entertainment Weekly party in the same outfit she wore on her interview. Chyna stood in the middle of the party looking like a complete square. She wore a white, wide lapel coat with black stripes, V-neck tee, black, pencil skirt and Casadei, strappy design, stiletto heels. Her outfit was super chic but it wasn't party attire at all. There was nothing sexy or eye-catching about her attire.

She looked like the head of the PTA. She wanted nothing more than to go home, shower and change into something fabulous but she wasn't there to party. She was there to work. Felicia had arrived thirty minutes prior and was working the room.

Chyna made sure she had everything a woman of her stature would need upon arrival. She had breath mints on deck, hand sanitizer, press powder and a glass of champagne prepared when she walked through the door. Chyna had a Cadillac Escalade outside waiting for when she was ready to leave. She even took the liberty to order Felicia and her husband dinner so they wouldn't be hungry at the end of the night.

Felicia was thoroughly impressed by Chyna's ability to be one step ahead of her needs. Chyna was killing her first day. She didn't want to be someone's errand girl but she was willing to do whatever she had to do to get into The Writers' Room. If Felicia wanted her to strip and run butt naked down Washington Boulevard, she would. If she wanted her to pussy pop on a handstand, she would. If Felicia told her to kidnap a kid, Chyna would be at the next schoolyard ready to catch a kid. Well, she wouldn't go that far but her hunger to write for the show was real.

Chyna watched as party-goers sipped champagne and mingled. She wanted to turn up so bad but she was on work mood. DJ Khaled was spinning classic hip hop records from the late 90's. Some of her favorite actors, actresses and artist were in the building. EJ Johnson, Zendaya, Jourdan Dunn and Omari Hardwick were all in attendance.

On several occasions Chyna almost fanned out and asked them for a selfie but she kept her composure.

Prayerfully, one day she'd be working with them. She didn't want to come across unprofessional. There was also a slew of athletes there but she didn't know any of their names. Chyna was just happy she'd gotten her life back on track. It felt extremely good to be drama free. The fuckboy repellent she'd sprayed all over herself had clearly worked. None of her old boos had bothered to call and bother her. They'd thankfully gotten the clue that she wasn't down for their shit anymore.

Nothing in this life was promised and Chyna wasn't going to spend another day doing dumb shit. She was gonna live every day to the fullest. She planned on vacationing in France one day and blowing a stack while shopping. She was over doing basic bitch things. Fuck going to the club and giving good pussy to unworthy niggas. Chyna was after money, power and respect. Getting fucked over by men who didn't know themselves, let alone what they wanted in a woman, wasn't an option anymore.

Chyna needed a sure thing, something tangible and real. She needed a man that was going to lift her up not tear her down with their confusion and lies. She wanted what Felicia had. Her husband would have to support her the way Felicia's did. The man Chyna ended up with had to be secure enough in himself that he could watch her spread her wings and fly and not feel threatened by her success.

Chyna had every intention on building an empire. She needed a confident man by her side that would help nurture and support her dream. Being a boss bitch wasn't easy. It was already hard enough for her and she hadn't achieved even a fraction of the success she craved.

Chyna scanned the room for Felicia. She didn't want to miss a beat in case she needed anything. She watched from afar as Felicia talked to a tall, chocolate brother in a Tom Ford suit. The man was magically delicious. He gave Chyna a 60-year-old Idris Elba vibe. She didn't know who he was but the man looked like a bag of money. Millions radiated off his skin. He commanded the whole room and looked like he could make or break a lot of careers. Chyna didn't fuck with older men but old man Elba could most definitely get it.

Felicia must've felt the same way because she smiled and giggled in his face like a schoolgirl. *That gotta be Mr. Abbot,* Chyna thought as Felicia flipped her hair for the tenth time. Chyna prayed to be as in love with her husband after 20 years of marriage. Felicia and her husband had major chemistry and couldn't keep their hands off each other. When they thought no one was looking, Chyna peeped them stealing an affectionate touch here and there. She found it to be sweet and endearing how much Felicia loved her husband.

Well at least someone is crazy in love, Chyna looked around feeling like the odd girl out. She wanted a boo thang too. For a minute, she contemplated hitting Carlos up but quickly dismissed the idea. *No bitch! Your pussy is closed for business.* There would be no dropping it like it was hot for her. Besides, Carlos didn't want her anyway. He'd chosen fake-ass Kim K over her.

She had to forget Carlos ever existed. At the end of the night, Chyna was going home. She had leftover beef and broccoli and an ice cold Cranberry Grape Ocean Spray in the refrigerator waiting on her. She would pig-out and take her ass to bed. Plus, her feet were killing her from standing up all day. Chyna couldn't ride a dick that night if Anna Nicole Smith came down from heaven and helped her herself. Finished with her conversation, Felicia and her husband walked over to Chyna. Chyna immediately prepared herself for the next task.

"Chyna, you had a very successful first day. I'm very pleased," Felicia smiled, satisfied.

"Thank you. Is there anything else I can do for you today?" Chyna asked ready for anything.

"No, I'm about to head home; but before I do, I would like you to meet the president of programming for HBO, Warren Smith."

"It's a pleasure to meet you, sir." Chyna extended her hand shocked that the gentleman wasn't Felicia's husband.

"Nice to meet you too," Warren shook her hand, firmly.

"Chyna's trying to work her way onto my Jr. Writing Team." Felicia informed Warren.

"Oh, you're a writer?" Warren asked shocked.

"Yes, sir. Hopefully one day I'll be a show runner and EP like Felicia," Chyna replied unsure of what to make of their relationship.

In front of her they acted like mere colleagues. All of the flirtatious behavior they'd exhibited had completely gone out of the window.

"With hard work, determination and Felicia by your side, you'll get there," Warren assured.

"Well, I'm going to call it a night. Good job, again, Chyna. I'll see you bright and early Monday morning," Felicia said, firmly.

"Yes, ma'am. Bright and early." Chyna saluted her like a soldier.

"It was nice meeting you, Chyna." Warren said goodbye.

Thoroughly confused as to what she'd just witnessed, Chyna watched as Warren escorted Felicia to the door. They stood and talked for another minute then Felicia left by herself. *Bitch, you are obviously trippin'. They are not fuckin' around,* she thought grabbing a glass of champagne. Chyna had to have one glass before she left. Chugging it down, she placed the empty glass back on the table and headed out herself.

The freezing cold November air hit her smack dab in the face as she stepped outside. Chyna wrapped herself up in her coat and called a cab. As she waited for an operator to get on the line, she spotted the car she'd ordered for Felicia circle back around the building and park at the end of the corner. Chyna figured Felicia needed her to do something else so she started walking towards the car.

Then abruptly, she stopped walking and crouched down behind a bush. She couldn't let Felicia know she'd caught Warren getting in the back of the car with her. *Oh, they're most definitely fuckin',* Chyna thought as they pulled off.

"Chyna?" She heard a deep male voice say from behind.

Scared out of her mind, she leaped to her feet and turned around. L.A. furrowed his brows and looked at her like she was nuts. The long-legged, blonde, Sports Illustrated model he was with eyed her like she was a crazy woman as well.

"You okay?" He stared at her suspiciously.

Chyna tried to remember the English language but only gibberish filled her mind. L.A. looked beautiful under the night's sky. She'd always found him attractive but that night there was something different about him. It was as if she was seeing him for the first time. There was a look of intensity in his eyes that scared her. It was almost like he could see into her soul. Chyna felt naked before him.

"Chyna?" He called out. "You a'ight?"

"Yeah, I umm," She looked around lost for words. "Lost my contact." She winked her right eye profusely and pretended to search around the ground.

L.A. knew she was lying but decided not to put her on blast.

"You leaving the party?" He pointed back at the building.

"Yeah, I'm about to head home and turn in for the night," she replied looking over at the girl he was with. "You gon' introduce me to your friend?" Chyna looked her up-and-down with an attitude.

"My bad," L.A. chuckled.

He'd completely forgotten about his date.

"Emily, this is my homegirl Chyna. Chyna, this is Emily."

Homegirl, Chyna turned up her face. *Nigga, you been tryin' to get at me for months. Now I'm just your homegirl? Negro, please.*

"Hey," Chyna spoke dryly.

"Hi," Emily said sweetly. "I love your shoes. They're so cute."

"Thank you." Chyna rolled her eyes.

She tried not to hate the girl because she had no reason to but she couldn't stand the sight of her. She hated everything about her. She was too tall, too slim, too beautiful and far too close to L.A. *Why the hell is he here with her anyway,* she wondered. He was supposed to be at home pining after her. He'd said he was going to wait on her so why wasn't he waiting?

Sure, she'd told him they could only be friends but that didn't mean he could go out and date other people. Chyna should've been the one on his arm. Not this Gigi Hadid looking bitch. L.A. had her completely fucked up. It wasn't fair that he seriously had her rethinking her views on dating. Seeing him with someone else bothered her immensely.

"I'm late meeting someone but you sure you don't want to come and have a drink with us?" L.A. quizzed, hoping she'd say yes.

Is this nigga stupid? What the fuck I look like? This ain't an episode of Full House. I ain't Kimmy Gibbler. I'm no one's third wheel, Chyna scowled.

"I wish I would," she replied instead. "Have a good night." She stormed past him upset.

"Hold up, wait!" L.A. called after her. "Emily, I'll be right back."

L.A. ran and caught up with Chyna.

"What's wrong wit' you?" He stopped her and made her face him.

"Really, L.A? You really dating a white girl named Emily?" Chyna declared, self-righteously.

"Oh, so you can date a white man but I can't date a white girl? Let me find out you're a racist," he laughed.

"I don't see nothin' funny." Chyna folded her arms across her chest defiantly.

"Seems to me like you're a li'l bit jealous. You said you didn't want me, remember?"

"I know what I said." Chyna tried to play it off like she was unfazed by him being with another woman.

"Admit it. You want me." He said with an intense look of desire in his eye.

Everything in Chyna wanted to give in and let him have her but she couldn't let L.A. get the best of her. She wished she could let her guard down but fear of the unknown kept her at bay.

"Goodnight, L.A." She turned and left him standing there.

L.A. sucked his teeth. He knew the feelings he had for Chyna should be long gone. But every time he saw her golden-brown face, feelings reemerged. No other woman had this kind of effect on him. He couldn't see himself going the distance with another girl. Chyna changed his perception of forever. He saw it whenever he looked into her eyes.

Somehow she'd captured his heart and rearranged it. All he wanted was to please, kiss and make her happy. L.A. didn't know what to do. He was by no means a slouch. He had the world at his fingertips. He was Lucas Abbot for god's sake. The two-time, NBA champion and $100 million man. He could have any woman on the planet he desired but he wanted her.

"YOU'RE LIKE A VITAL ORGAN; I CAN'T LIVE WITHOUT YOU." - STACY BARTHE FEAT. FRANK OCEAN, "WITHOUT YOU"

CHAPTER THIRTEEN

A strong Jack and Coke called Chyna's name as she stood lifeless under the shower head. A waterfall of steaming hot water cascaded over her face, shoulders, breasts and thighs. If she could've stayed there forever under the comforting water she would've. Being alone in the solace of her bathroom was her only escape. It was the only place she could be herself. In front of everyone, including India, she had to pretend to be upbeat and happy but she wasn't. Chyna hurt like everyone too.

No matter how hard she tried to find peace, chaos swarmed around her. She tried to run and hide from it but it always seemed to find her. She needed a moment to breathe. She had to find a way to catch herself before she fell into a deep abyss. She couldn't afford to become bitter, angry or depressed but she felt it coming on.

All she wanted was unwavering, unconditional love. Was that too much to ask for? Why was it so hard for her to find her soul mate? She was 34 years old for God's sake.

You couldn't have told Chyna when she was in her 20's that she wouldn't be married and on baby #2 by now. Here she was in her mid-thirties still a single mom with no shot at real love in sight.

One of her worst fears was to end up alone. She didn't want to be like her mother, Diane, or all the other single women in her family. She'd give anything to have a complete family with an apple tree and a four-door car with a baby seat in the rear. She and India deserved to have a happy ending. But from the looks of things, Chyna would never have her happily ever after. Tyreik was married, Carlos was in love with Bellamy, L.A. had found someone new and Asif was in denial about being gay.

Chyna couldn't win for losing. She hadn't predicted that L.A. would move on so quickly. He made it seem like he was really digging her. Chyna chalked his words of affection up to typical fuckboy talk. She couldn't put her faith in none of these niggas. That didn't stop her from feeling some type of way. She didn't like seeing him with another chick.

It pissed her off. It should've been her with him. Chyna wasn't the type of chick to put her feelings out on the table but she liked L.A. She wanted to be the one he took on dates.

She wanted to be the one he thought of during the day. She wanted to be the one he pined after. But if she took it there with him, he would end up catching feelings and she would hurt him. Chyna couldn't have that on her conscious. L.A. was a good guy. He deserved more than for her to fuck him over.

Plus, she knew if she ever got a taste of the D, she'd probably become addicted. Bomb-ass dick and Chyna didn't mix. She always became lovesick after getting good dick. No, Chyna was going to stay away from L.A. and his potentially amazing penis. As the water from the shower went from hot to cold, Chyna examined her hands. Her fingertips were starting to shrivel up like raisins. It was time for her to get out. Mentally and physically restored, she turned off the water, grabbed her towel and got out. She couldn't hide from the world forever. She had to face her reality.

After drying off she massaged her entire body with scented lotion. It was a Victoria Secret Pink collection kind of night. Chyna needed something bright and colorful to lift her spirits. She threw on a pink and white polka dot matching tank top and campus short set. In desperate need of exfoliation, she placed her favorite clay mask all over her face. Skincare was important to Chyna now that she was getting older.

It only took the mask fifteen minutes to work its magic. Chyna washed the substance off her face as the sound of someone banging on her door startled her. She wanted to open her eyes and run to see who it was but she couldn't risk getting any of the clay mask in her eye. Chyna quickly washed the rest away and patted her face dry with a towel.

Clueless to who would have the balls to pop up at her house and cause a ruckus, she ran down the steps. As she made her way down, the unexpected visitor banged on the door again and rang the doorbell at the same time. India stood outside her bedroom door visibly shaken.

"Who is that at the door?" Chyna asked mad as hell.

"Some white man," India shrugged her shoulders.

Chyna knew exactly who it was then.

"I got it. Go back in your room and close the door," Chyna ordered.

Unsure if her mom could handle whoever was at the door by herself, India eyed her mother apprehensively before doing as she was told. Chyna waited until India's door was all the way closed before she peeked through the blinds. Carlos leaned against her doorframe with his face pressed up against the glass. He was so drunk he didn't even notice her staring at him.

"Chyna!" He rang the bell several times. "Come on, baby! Open up! I need to talk to you!" He knocked again.

Fed up with his nonsense, Chyna unlocked the door and swung it open. Carlos stood up abruptly and looked at her with glassy, red eyes. He looked like he'd been drinking for hours.

"What the hell is wrong with you? What do you want? My daughter is here," she hissed.

"I needed to see you." He pleaded with his eyes.

Carlos couldn't stay away a minute longer. Ever since the bonfire he'd been drinking his self to death to stop the memories of her. Visions of her face haunted on him daily. He missed the way they used to lay up, sex and blow dank. There was no fighting it anymore. They were meant to be together. She was his rib. Looking at old pictures of her and stalking her Instagram just wasn't enough anymore. He had to see her.

"I missed you." He rushed in and took her by the face before she could protest.

Carlos reeked of liquor but she was so in love with him that the foul stench didn't bother her at all.

"Chyna, I fucked up." He held her face with both of his hands and stared deep into her eyes.

Tears clouded his vision. Anguish was written all over his face.

"I should've never did you the way I did. I regret it every day. But I need you to understand that I wasn't ready the day you gave me your heart. I was in a lot of pain," he slurred his words. "I was fallin' apart. I was miserable as fuck. My son dying nearly killed me, Chyna. I never thought

I'd be able to love again but all I do is wonder about you. Baby, I can't live without you." He let a single tear trickle down his cheek.

"I love you." He confessed, placing his lips upon hers.

Chyna broke the kiss and snatched her head back.

"Don't lie to me," she warned.

"I'm not. I love you. You're the only one for me." Carlos rested his forehead against hers.

Chyna could feel her spirit leave her chest then re-enter through his kiss. She felt reborn again. This was what she'd longed to hear. *He loves me,* she smiled as tears filled her eyes. *He loves me. Me.*

"Please, just give me another chance. I promise, I'll make it better," he begged.

There was no way Chyna could say no. She loved the man standing before her. All she ever wanted was for him to give her his heart. Now he was finally ready. She couldn't possibly pass up the opportunity to have her fairytale dream come true. Since the day they met he'd taken control of her heart and never let it go. She wanted to build with him. Together they could create the impossible. They'd hit rock bottom so there was nowhere for them to go but up. It had to work between them this time.

"Come on, let's go upstairs." She helped him up the steps.

Carlos tried to keep up with her but all of the alcohol he'd consumed altered his ability to walk straight. He stumbled up several steps. Chyna had to lift him up and help him so they both wouldn't fall. It took all of the strength she had just to get him on the second floor. Chyna stood panting heavily dreading going up another flight of stairs.

"Hold up, baby." Carlos let go of her and took several short breaths.

His body was boiling hot and his stomach curled.

"Oh God. Oh no." He drooled, feeling nauseated.

"What's wrong?" Chyna rubbed his back, concerned.

"I don't feel good." Carlos swayed from side-to-side.

"C'mon, let's get you upstairs," she urged, trying to get him to walk.

"I can't." He replied barely able to catch his breath. "I gotta throw up." His olive skin turned red.

"Ok, let me get you upstairs so you won't throw up on my living room floor!" Chyna tried to push him towards the steps.

"I'm not gonna make it!" Carlos held his mouth with the palm of his hand, looking for a place to url.

"You better make it!" Chyna screeched.

"I can't!" Carlos bent over and spewed vomit from his mouth.

Chunks of food and liquor splattered on the floor and bounced up onto Chyna's legs and feet. After that, everything went silent.

"You did not just throw up on me?" She closed her eyes tight and said a prayer to God.

Hesitant, she opened her eyes and saw pink globs of vomit dripping from her legs.

"Lord Jesus, I'ma faint." She said ready to pass out.

"I'm so sorry. Baby, I'm sorry." Carlos reached out for her.

Chyna scooted back so he couldn't touch her.

"Mom! Is everything okay?" India called up the steps, worried.

"Yes, baby; Mama's okay! Go back into your room!"

When Chyna thought the coast was clear, she turned her attention back to the drunken fool.

"I never thought I would go to jail for murder but, Carlos... I'm gonna kill you!" She slapped him repeatedly in the arm.

"Baby, I'm sorry." He responded sincerely.

"Get your ass upstairs, get undressed and get in the shower! I'll be up there in a second!"

"Chyna, baby... listen—"

"NOW!" She pointed, vehemently.

Carlos tiredly climbed up the steps using his hands and feet. Completely disgusted, Chyna wiped her legs and feet off with a paper towel. She cleaned off the floor too then mopped it with Pine-Sol and hot water. Once the floor was spic and span clean, she raced up the steps. Chyna couldn't risk Carlos drowning himself in the tub. She'd threatened to kill him but she didn't want him to die for real.

She was genuinely happy he was there. She'd wanted him in her house and her bedroom for months. Despite the vomiting, she cherished each and every second they got to spend together. Chyna entered her bathroom. All of Carlos' clothes were sprawled on the floor. He'd done exactly what she'd told him and got in the shower. Chyna picked up his clothes and threw them in the washing machine.

Needing to shower herself, Chyna locked the door behind her and stripped down naked. Quietly, she got in the shower with him. Carlos stood under the shower head just as she had less than an hour before. Chyna drunk in every part of him. His muscular back begged to be kissed. Chyna leaned forward and wrapped her arms around his waist. Carlos stood up straight and turned to face her.

He hadn't been that close to her in months. It felt great to have her skin pressed against his. Chyna was the love of his life. He loved her to the moon and back. He wanted to give her everything she ever needed and desired. He hated that he made her upset and disappointed her at times. Seeing her happy was all that mattered to him. Not loving her wasn't any option anymore. She held his heart in the palm of her hand. Life without her wasn't living. He'd suffered long enough. Carlos was fully ready to surrender his mind, heart and soul to her.

"You still love me?" He traced his thumb across her cheek.

"Not right now I don't," she quipped still mad that he'd thrown up on her.

"Stop lying. You love me." He said as more of a statement than a question.

There was no escaping the truth. Chyna's heart wouldn't allow her to tell another lie.

"You know I do." She spoke barely above a whisper. "I will always love you." She passionately kissed his lips.

Instantly, she became lost in each flicker of his tongue. Needing to feel every part of her, Carlos lifted her legs up over his arms. He ached to be inside her. As soon as his wet, hard dick entered her slit, he felt at home. Carlos gazed deep into her brown eyes as she cried out in ecstasy. He understood her emotions. He was overwhelmed too. Loving her was intense and complicated but it felt so right. This was exactly where he belonged. After that night, he'd never leave her again.

Hot water cascaded over their bodies as they made love. Carlos licked and sucked her neck. Chyna missed him so much. She had to taste him. Easing off his dick, she took him in her mouth. The first lick tasted like heaven. Chyna tried to fit all of him in her mouth. Carlos' long, pink rod was hard against the taste buds of her tongue. She was so wet. Carlos ran his fingers through her hair. Chyna was sucking the shit out of his dick.

"Fuck," he groaned on the brink of exploding. "Stand up, baby."

Chyna eased off her knees and turned around. Carlos knew exactly how she liked it. Water streamed down her back as he fucked her hard from behind. Chyna tried her best not to scream. No one could fuck her like Carlos could. His dick was a perfect fit. Chyna pressed her hands against the shower wall and tried to hold on.

"Oh my God. Fuck me." She moaned as his pelvis slapped against her butt cheeks.

This was the fix she needed. This was what her body had been craving.

"God damn. Oh my God," she whimpered. "Oh shit. Ah yes. Baby."

Carlos cupped her breasts. He'd never been so hard in his life. Only Chyna could make him feel this way.

"This my pussy." He whispered in her ear.

"Oh my God, yes this is your pussy." Chyna's eyes rolled to the back of her head.

"I love this pussy."

"Carlos!" Chyna gasped, cumming. "This dick feels so good."

"Don't you ever give my pussy away. You hear me?" He gripped her neck.

"Yes!" Chyna climaxed, cumming long and hard.

An hour later, Carlos lie sound asleep in her bed. Chyna lay next to him and watched as he slept. She could sit there and watch him for hours and never get bored. At that very moment, she had it all. She had her man back, was working for her idol and her daughter was good. What more could a girl ask for? Life was fantastic. Gently, she reached over and played with his hair. Carlos stirred a little in his sleep but didn't wake.

Chyna placed her nose against his skin and inhaled his scent. His scent was as intoxicating as the smell of a newborn baby. She loved him so much it was a tad bit scary. It had gotten to a point where her happiness depended on whether or not they were together. Chyna knew she couldn't live that way. No human being should have that much control over her emotions but she couldn't help herself. Carlos was all she'd ever wanted.

She wished she could spend every day of her life curled up in bed beside him but reality struck when his cellphone started to vibrate. Chyna looked at Carlos to see if he'd wake but he didn't. He was in such a deep sleep, he was snoring. After several rings, the caller hung up then called back again. This time Chyna couldn't help but to look and see who it was. It was of no surprise that the caller was Bellamy.

It was after midnight and Carlos hadn't come home yet. If she was in Bellamy's shoes she'd be blowing up his phone too. But Chyna wasn't in her shoes. She wasn't the frantic girlfriend at home wondering where her man was. She was the one he was lying next to. She didn't have a care in the world. She had nothing to worry about. The man they both loved was right there with her.

Not one to give up, Bellamy hung up and called him again. Chyna tried her best not to jump aboard the petty express but she couldn't help herself. Payback was a bitch and Bellamy deserved everything that was about to come to her.

"Hello?" Chyna picked up on the fourth ring.

Bellamy took the phone away from her ear and looked to make sure she'd dialed the right number. When she realized she had, her heart stopped.

"Who is this?" She snapped.

"Hey, Bellamy, girl. How are you? This is Chyna, Carlos rebound," she spoke sweetly.

Bellamy swallowed the huge lump in her throat and tried not to explode.

"Put Carlos on the phone," she demanded.

"I'm sorry. I won't be able to do that. You see... he's asleep right now... next to me and it would be so rude of me to wake him. You understand that, don't you?" Chyna spoke condescendingly.

Bellamy held the phone, speechless. She figured that Carlos was with her but now that her suspicions had been confirmed, rage seeped through her veins.

"Chyna, you are as tired as a Coogi sweater. Put my husband on the phone," Bellamy demanded.

"Ex-husband, honey," Chyna corrected her.

"Carlos will always be mine. He's never going to leave me for you. You do know that, right? You're not marriage material. No man wants a woman who has been used and abused. You're worthless. Your pussy is trash. You're a joke. The only reason Carlos keeps coming back to you is because he knows he can." Bellamy tried to tear her down.

Chyna wanted to act like her words didn't sting but they did. Her biggest fear was that she wasn't good enough to be wifey material. There was no way in hell she was going to let Bellamy know she'd hit a sore spot. It was time for Chyna to murder and destroy.

"Bellamy, darling, why are you so bitter? I mean, you are pathetic and that's coming from someone who likes wearing white after Labor Day. Honey, I am the least of your concerns. You need to be worried about your dick in the booty-ass brother and why he has a hard-on for you."

"What? My brother isn't gay!" Bellamy fought the truth.

"Oh girl, your brother is gay. He is gayer than the rainbow flag. Ask him why he can't keep a girlfriend," Chyna shot.

Bellamy held the phone unable to respond. Once again, Chyna had hit her with a one hitter quitter.

"Now you have a goodnight, sweetie. Sleep tight, okay?" Chyna ended the call, grinning from ear-to-ear.

"WHAT A WICKED WAY TO TREAT THE GIRL THAT LOVES YOU." –BEYONCÉ, "HOLD UP"

CHAPTER FOURTEEN

Unable to sleep, Chyna sat Indian-style and did research on how to write a spec script. It was almost 4:00am but she had to learn the blueprint on how to format one before she started working. When she turned her spec into Felicia it had to be 100% on point. There was no way she was going to fuck up twice. Her career as a television writer depended on her nailing this.

She couldn't leave anything up to chance. Chyna was going to put her all into the spec and leave the rest up to God's will. Carlos lay passed out underneath the covers as she worked. This was what she wanted the rest of her life to look like. She hadn't felt this full in a long while. She prayed to God that the feeling would last an eternity.

Carlos stirred in his sleep and yawned. He had to pee. Chyna took her attention off her laptop and looked over at him. She wasn't going to be caught off guard this time, if he needed to throw up. She already had a trash can by the bed just in case. Carlos turned his head in her direction and opened his eyes. Chyna was the first thing he saw. He thanked God for the blessing. He'd wanted to wake up to her face for months but unfortunate circumstances kept getting in the way. Carlos gazed at her and smiled. He was still hungover but was thinking much clearer.

"Well look who decided to wake up," Chyna teased, ruffling his hair.

"Come here." He reached out for her and pulled her close.

Chyna uncrossed her legs and lay facing him. Carlos caressed her face with his hand and pushed her hair back. With or without makeup, she was stunning. Her hypnotizing brown eyes and deep dimples were works of art. He could stare at her till he was old and gray. He'd always find new things to admire. Being with her put his heart at ease.

He felt like he could breathe again. With Bellamy, things were always strained and tense. He was tired of trying to make their relationship work. They'd tried and failed but leaving her alone for good was easier said than done. They'd known each other half their lives. If he left her he'd not only be breaking up with her but her family as well. He'd grown extremely close to her mother and father and vice versa.

His parents loved Bellamy and were crushed by their divorce. Both sets of parents were elated when they decided to get back together. Carlos couldn't let them down again. It would break their hearts. History, love and loyalty is what kept him tied to Bellamy. But what was he to do when he wasn't happy? The woman he held in his arms was who he truly wanted.

With Chyna, he was free to be himself. He didn't have to put on a front to appease her. They had so much in common. She understood him. With her it was always a good time. Chyna was fun and down for whatever. She made it difficult to love her at times but he wasn't easy to crack open either.

Chyna was the mirror image of him which was a blessing and a curse. She knew how to get under his skin like no other. But none of that mattered as he placed his nose on her neck and inhaled the sweet scent of her skin.

Chyna cracked up laughing and tried to back away as he bit at her neck like a dog.

"Uh ah, come back. You ain't going nowhere." He pulled her back and tickled her stomach.

"Stop!" She gasped in tears from laughing so hard.

Carlos eased tickling her and rolled out of the bed.

"I gotta take a piss." He announced heading towards the bathroom.

Spent from his tickle attack, Chyna lay on her back trying to catch her breath. *Lord, please let him be mine,* she prayed as he returned. Chyna eyed him lustfully as he walked back over to the bed. Carlos was built like a god. His body was magnificent. The tattoos that adorned his chest, arms, hands and legs were added bonuses. The biggest plus of them all was his ten inch, meaty dick. Chyna zeroed in on it and licked her bottom lip. She would gladly take him in her mouth again if he asked. Carlos caught her staring at his dick and grinned.

"What you lookin' at?" He grabbed it and held it in his hand.

"My friend." Chyna flirted.

"You wanna tell yo' friend, hi?" Carlos stood on the side of the bed and stroked his dick.

Chyna sunk her teeth into the flesh of her lip. She could see herself crawling over to him and taking his cock in her warm mouth. Chyna wanted to devour him but remembered India was two floors down. If she and Carlos got started, there would be no stopping, and being quiet this time wasn't an option.

"Don't tempt me," she responded instead.

"You wack." Carlos joked waving her off. "Where my clothes at?" He looked around the room.

"Right there." She pointed to a pile of clothes on her chaise lounge. "I washed them."

"My bad for throwing up on you." Carlos put on his boxer/briefs.

"Yeah, let's not do that ever again."

"I ain't been this drunk in a minute." He combed his hair back with his hand.

"Where were you coming from?"

"Bar Louie." He sat on the edge of the bed and grabbed his phone.

Carlos checked his phone and saw a slew of missed calls from Bellamy.

"Fuck." He said out loud to himself.

He did not feel like hearing her mouth about him not coming home. She'd sent him over twenty messages. Carlos scrolled through them all. The first set started off pleasant and sweet. She asked where he was and when he was coming home. Then the text turned frantic. She wondered if he was hurt and if she should call the police. Frantic then went to ballistic. Carlos was every low-life son-of-a-bitch in the book.

<u><Messages   Bellamy   Details</u>

Are you really with that slut bitch, right now?

Since you wanna lay up with whores instead of coming home, stay your ass over there with Chyna!

I hope you're having fun. I hope you're enjoying yourself.

I swear to God, Carlos, I hate you!

Carlos screwed up his face. He was pretty drunk but he didn't remember talking to Bellamy at all that night.

"I ain't answer my phone. Did you answer my phone?" He looked over his shoulder at Chyna, confused.

"Yeah, I answered our phone." Chyna said with a smirk.

"You did what?" He turned all the way around to face her.

Carlos didn't find her funny at all.

"I answered our phone." Chyna spoke slowly so he could understand every word that was coming out of her mouth.

"Why would you do that?"

"'Cause she kept on callin'." Chyna stressed with an attitude.

"But you still shouldn't have touched my phone. Both of y'all need to stop with this dumb, tit-for-tat bullshit. It's gettin' on my fuckin' nerves." He stood up, pissed.

Carlos was sick and tired of the constant fighting between Chyna and Bellamy.

"Excuse you?" Chyna said appalled by his choice of words.

"You heard me. You shouldn't have answered my fuckin' phone. Why would you answer my phone when you knew it was her? You on some petty shit. You need to grow up."

"I need to grow up? No muthafucka, you need to grow up! You the one playing games. You're the one that showed up on my doorstep talking about you love me. I ain't seek you out! You obviously still got feelings for her or you wouldn't be trippin' off me answering your phone. Obviously, y'all still got something going on that she's blowin' up your phone all night!"

Carlos charged across the room and got in her face.

"I'm in your bed sleep!" He pounded his fist against his chest. "Why do you even give a fuck who's callin' me? I tell you I love you and you trippin' off who callin' my phone after I told you how I feel about you! So why does her callin' even matter? Grow up, Chyna, or this shit between me and you ain't gon' work! Stop actin' like a fuckin' kid all the time. Grow up. Ain't nobody got time for these li'l girl-ass games you be playin'."

"I'm a kid? I'm a li'l girl?" She cocked her head back. "But you the muthafucka that came knockin' on my door. Yeah, I'm a kid; more like an infant, baby type," She stuck her thumb in her mouth and sucked it.

"See, that's what I'm talkin' about! You do dumb, kid shit." Carlos shook his head angrily.

"I tried to tell you." She laughed not giving a fuck about his attitude. "So, since I'm a kid." She got up and walked over to the chaise lounge and grabbed his clothes. "And I get on your nerves so much... how about you go home to your wife?!" She threw the clothes at him.

"My ex-wife!" He corrected her.

"I don't give a fuck who that bitch is. That bitch could be Michelle Obama for all I care," Chyna spat. "You and yo' phone ain't gotta be around me. Y'all can go home to your ex-wife! And how she know you ain't at home? Y'all stay together?" Chyna questioned afraid of his answer.

"No," Carlos lied.

If he told Chyna the truth, he knew she'd be done with him for good.

"Let me find out you lying. You know what? It don't even matter. Just go home."

"You really call yo'self being mad at me? I'm the one that should be mad at you! You fucked my brother-in-law!" Carlos shot furiously.

"I sure did and what?" Chyna dared.

"See, that's what I'm talkin' about. Your mouth is fuckin' crazy. You say dumb shit but then you wanna cry and tell me you love me and how much you wanna be with me. Get the fuck outta here, man. You try and act like the victim but you're just as guilty as me!" Carlos barked.

"Are you fuckin' kidding me? You sat there and led me on all summer, made me fall in love with you, then you fuck me, break up with me and tell me you were married and had a dead baby, but I'm wrong? Yeah okay, Carlos. Try that bullshit with somebody else."

"Say one more thing about my son," he warned.

"Mom, are you okay?" India asked from the bottom of the steps.

"Yes, baby; Mama's okay," she lied. "Go back to bed."

Oh my God, Chyna thought. *It's happening again.* Life was repeating itself. She'd been here before. Carlos was mirroring Tyreik. Chyna couldn't believe she'd found herself in the same position with a new man.

"You gotta go." She shook her head. "I'm not about to argue with you or anybody else. You ain't even my damn man. Take yo' ass home and drive Bellamy insane."

"You a straight kid, man." Carlos shook his head in disbelief as he put on his clothes.

"I'll be that." Chyna sat back down on her bed and resumed working. "Don't say shit else to me; don't come back to my house until you figure out what the fuck you wanna do."

She wasn't going to let Carlos fuck up her night. She shouldn't have ever let him in her crib in the first place. Fully dressed, he grabbed his keys and headed for the door.

"Lock the door on the way out." Chyna said not bothering to look up from her laptop.

"You stupid, man," Carlos shook his head and left without saying another word.

How did I get here, Bellamy thought as tears slid down her face. It was going on 5:00am and Carlos still wasn't home. She didn't want to lose her cool but if he kept this shit up she was sure to fuck him and his side-bitch up. Bellamy knew things between them were shaky but she didn't know they were experiencing a full on earthquake. With each second that passed and he didn't walk through the door, a deadly pain pierced her organs. The only time she'd experienced a pain like this was when she went through the death of her child.

Carlos was a firsthand witness to her turmoil. He saw how she almost shriveled up and died. He saw the galloons of tears she cried. He watched as she lay in bed unable to move a muscle. He saw her spazz out and lose her mind. He knew just how far down the rabbit hole she could go. It made no sense to her that he would risk taking her back to such a dark place.

She'd loved him since the 11th grade. Back then he was kind, humble and thoughtful of her feelings. He used to do anything to put a smile on her face. He hated to see her cry or be upset. Now, years later, he was the cause of her pain. When they were younger, Bellamy adored him despite his shortcomings. She looked past the fact that he was poor and came from the projects. The other girls in their class used to make fun of him. To them, he was nothing but an awkward, shy, skinny, Italian, wanna-be that could dribble a basketball. He was nowhere near the confident man he was now.

Every guy in school wanted Bellamy, including his homeboy, L.A., who on paper was her perfect match. They both were extremely attractive and came from well-to-do families. Bellamy had her pick of the litter but she chose Carlos when no one else wanted him. She saw his potential. She knew Carlos would grow up to be great and her prediction was right. He was the man now. You couldn't tell him he wasn't the shit.

After making a name for himself and growing into his looks, he became a cocky, arrogant, son-of-a-bitch. Chicks started flocking to him and homeboy lost his mind. Bellamy quickly became an afterthought. He completely forgot about the fact that she'd loved him before the money, cars and tattoos.

She was the one that groomed him, nurtured, motivated and supported him. She was his biggest fan. His biggest cheerleader. She went through hell for years to give him a child so their family could be complete. She was the one that suffered through getting poked and prodded. Now none of that mattered and she'd morphed from his dream girl to a regular bitch off the street.

Bellamy didn't know when shit flipped but she wasn't here for Carlos disrespecting her and shit. He had her completely fucked up if he thought she was going to sit back and let him treat her this way. Bellamy had far better things to do than to be sitting up crying over a lying, cheating-ass man but the tears wouldn't stop. They just kept coming.

She felt like a fool for wasting her tears on him but she hurt like hell. It was becoming abundantly clear that they might not be able to salvage their relationship. She still loved him but from Carlos' actions, it didn't seem like he still loved her. Bellamy refused to become a weak, sham of a woman but piece by piece she felt herself falling apart. She wanted the old Carlos back. She missed the way he used to adore her. When he looked at her now, she saw nothing but anguish and disdain.

He acted like she got on his nerves. *What have I done to make him treat me this way,* her chest heaved up-and-down. All she ever did was try to love him. Was this her consolation prize? Bellamy wanted answers. It was 5:27am when Carlos finally walked through the door. Bellamy would never forget the time. It would forever be etched in her brain. Using the back of her hand, she quickly wiped her face.

Carlos strolled into their bedroom casually and placed his keys down as if nothing was wrong. He didn't even bother to say hello. He walked past the bed and began taking off his clothes like she wasn't even there. This infuriated Bellamy even more. She was so enraged her whole entire being began to shake. The disrespect was real. She wanted to leap off the bed and attack him like she was a crazed spider monkey.

"Who the fuck do you think I am?" She squinted her eyes and glared at him.

"Look, I know you're mad but can we please do this later?" Carlos said exasperated.

After arguing with Chyna he didn't have any energy left to fight with Bellamy too.

"Excuse you?" She replied taken aback by his lack of compassion.

Incapable of controlling herself, she rose from the bed and got in his face.

"You really think you gon' walk your ass up in here at five o'clock in the morning after being with that BITCH all night and I'm not gon' say nothing?" She pointed her finger in his face. "Are you stupid or are you dumb?" She mushed him on the side of his head.

"Yo, chill." Carlos caught her hand and forcefully pushed it away.

"No, bitch, you chill!" Bellamy said ready to throw down. "Who do you think you are? I smell that raggedy bitch's perfume all over you! Like... what have I ever done to you 'cause you act like you hate me? Do you still blame me for Dash's death?" She couldn't help but cry.

"No," Carlos replied truthfully.

He hated that she felt that way.

"What is it then? 'Cause I don't deserve this. I would never do what you did to me tonight," she sobbed uncontrollably. "You wanna know why? 'Cause I love you but you don't love me. You love her. Don't you?" Bellamy held her breath waiting for his reply.

"Yeah." Carlos responded truthfully, unable to give her any eye contact.

He couldn't risk seeing her heart break.

"Why are you with me then?" She died to know.

"'Cause I love you too," he shouted.

"Well isn't that sweet," Bellamy shot sarcastically. "You can't have your cake and eat it too, muthafucka. You ain't gon' play ping pong with my fuckin' emotions. You can't keep doing this to me. When you want me, you want me and when you don't, you don't. That's not fair to me. This constant tug of war on my heart is too much."

"I know." Carlos said feeling like a piece of shit.

Bellamy didn't deserve what he was putting her through and neither did Chyna.

"Maybe we just need some space," he suggested.

"Uh ah," Bellamy shook her head. "We not doing no damn space. What, so you can be free to stick your dick in her without feeling guilty about it? I don't think so. I need to know; are we going to work this shit out or not? I need to know if everything we've been through is enough for me to hold onto you."

Bellamy felt dumb as fuck for trying to salvage their relationship but she loved him. She couldn't just up and leave Carlos without putting up a fight. He was all she knew. Staying was far less painful than ending up alone and living without him for good. Carlos didn't know what to say or do. He was honestly torn between staying and leaving. His heart constantly swayed between the two.

"It's fucked up but I don't know what I wanna do," he shrugged his shoulders, out of answers.

"Well, I'm not going to put up with this shit. You need to choose 'cause I'm not about to sit up here and let you cheat on me. You are not going to have me out here looking like no damn dummy. Figure out what the hell you want or else I'm leaving you."

"YOU IN TROUBLE, MA." –PHARRELL WILLIAMS FEAT.
SNOOP DOGG, "THAT GIRL"

CHAPTER FIFTEEN

Chyna had been with young dudes, Hindus, papas, Columbians who cut pies, thug ones, and hoodlums but none of them could keep her attention for long. She wasn't the kind of chick that was easily impressed. A man had to do a lot to get at her. Chyna wanted a thug who was intelligent too. A thoroughbred. She didn't have time to be dealing with dudes that didn't know what the hell they wanted out of life -- like Carlos.

She loved him dearly but babygirl needed a real man. Not some boy that was torn between two women. After she kicked him out, a week had gone by and they hadn't spoken. She didn't want to speak to him anyway. After the way he talked to her, she was good on talking to him for a while. She didn't have time for idle conversation or chit chat. They needed to get to the real.

Either they were gonna be together or not. He couldn't keep her heart tied up in a knot. She was Chyna Danea Black after all. Mad dudes of all different persuasions chased after her. But no, here she was stuck on stupid tripping off of him. *Fuck that,* Chyna took a sip of Moscato and shook her ass to Mobb Deep's The Infamous. She was at home alone on a Friday night and had just finished working on her spec.

Chyna felt good about the direction she was heading. She was in the beginning stages of writing the spec but was making good progress. Her first week being Felicia's errand girl was stressful as fuck. Felicia had her running all over St. Louis doing this and that. Chyna never had a minute to catch her breath. She hadn't worked this hard since her days at Shop-N-Save. She was honored at the end of the week when she was rewarded with being able to sit in on a session in The Writers' Room.

It was so dope to see how everyone vibed off each other. Felicia had built a solid crew of writers who were all different but had the same work ethic and desire to create a bomb-ass show. The sore neck, back and feet would all be worth it when she made it onto the Jr. writing staff. Until then, Chyna was going to enjoy her Friday night solo mission.

India was on a three-day, weekend vacay from school. She wouldn't see her till Monday afternoon. Chyna loved when she had her house to herself. When India wasn't around she could drink and smoke as much as she wanted. She could walk around butt-ass-naked, blast rap music and stay out till the crack of dawn.

Chyna liked the idea of being home alone but after a few hours the novelty wore off and she began to feel lonely. When India went away for a long period of time, it reminded Chyna that one day her baby would be gone for good and she'd have no one to come home to. The notion scared the shit out of her. She needed someone to fill the void of India not being around.

She needed some male attention. The bottle of Moscato she'd devoured had her feeling extra frisky. Chyna needed her back cracked immediately. Her fingers weren't enough. She was sick of suffering from dick depravation. Fucking Carlos after suffering from a drought wasn't enough. Chyna glanced over at her phone mischievously. There was only one man she wanted to see.

She knew in the morning she'd regret making the call but any logical thinking had gone out of the window after her third glass of wine. She had to see him. Despite their circumstances, she hadn't been able to take her mind off of him. Chyna dialed the number and placed the phone up to her ear. Butterflies filled her stomach.

"Hello?" He answered on the second ring.

Chyna heard a bunch of loud music in the background.

"I wanna see you." She said seductively. "Come over."

"A'ight."

"The door will be unlocked." She said before ending the call.

Chyna took a deep breath. She couldn't continue to play herself but what was one more bad decision going to hurt? The flesh was a powerful thing. Chyna's body was starving. She didn't take advantage of her booty call the last time they saw one another but now was the time. If she didn't have a taste of him now, she'd explode.

An hour later, after showering, she stood in front of her bathroom mirror tweaking her look when the sound of heavy steps caught her attention. He'd arrived. Chyna looked towards the stairs. Her heart skipped a beat as L.A. came up the steps. Homeboy looked good as fuck in a distressed, bleach-splattered baseball cap, Alexander Wang, leather, moto jacket, cream t-shirt, jeans and Tims.

A set of gold chains swung from his neck. A gold, diamond-encrusted Audemars watch gleamed from his wrist. He was delectable. She could only describe him as the perfect treat. Chyna took in the rose tattoo that bloomed across his Adam's apple as he neared her with a bottle of Ace of Spades in hand.

As soon as L.A. got the call from her, he left the club and headed over. He didn't give a fuck that it was 2:00am or that she'd obviously called him over for sex. He was willing to satisfy her needs. He'd meant it when he said he was going to wait on her. He didn't know what to expect when he walked into her crib but loved what he saw. His dick got hard on sight.

L.A. was shocked when he found her standing in the bathroom dressed scantily clad. Chyna turned to face him in a sheer, nude, crisscross, Agent Provocateur bra. Sheer suspenders that crossed over her flat, toned stomach were attached to a pair of silk stockings. Pale pink, French, floral-embroidered, sheer panties and nude, Louboutin "So Kate" heels finished off the barely-there ensemble.

L.A. took a swig of champagne as he towered over her. Chyna tried to play it cool like she wasn't scared but he could see the fear in her eyes. He couldn't blame her. L.A. was very intimidating. L.A. placed the bottle of Ace down on the sink. Chyna pushed his jacket off over his shoulders as he took off his hat then removed his shirt. No words were spoken as he stood before her shirtless in just his chains, jeans and Tims.

L.A. had been waiting months for this moment. He'd daydreamed about it several times. The things he was about to do to her body should be considered illegal. Chyna's butt was pressed up against the bathroom sink as he held the back of her head and bit her neck. L.A. was ready to lick her from head to toe. Chyna held on tight as he lifted her up and placed her on top of the sink. She'd become his prisoner.

After that night, he planned on never letting her go. His face was buried in her neck as his hands roamed her hips and thighs. Chyna reached down to feel the length of him. L.A.'s dick stretched across his thigh. Chyna nearly came from just touching it. She was saturated and wet. L.A. was assaulting her neck with his tongue. Slowly, he made his way over to her luscious, full breasts.

He didn't show her erect nipples any mercy. They were his for the taking. Chyna arched her back and moaned. She knew fucking L.A. was going to be good but homeboy was proving himself to be a beast. As she called out for God, he poured champagne all over her breasts then placed a trail of wet kisses down her stomach. Chyna grinned as champagne bubbles popped on her chest. Pulling her panties to the side, L.A. buried his face into her eager, wet pussy.

Hungrily, he licked her fast. L.A. attacked her pussy with vigor. His tongue slid between her ass cheeks, leaving her unable to speak. Chyna gasped for air. Before she knew it, an orgasm so intense it made her cry roared throughout her body. Chyna had never experienced an orgasm so powerful before. Every drop of her was on his tongue.

Chyna gazed into his eyes and dropped to her knees. She'd fantasized about how he would taste for months. Sexily, she unzipped his jeans while never taking her eyes off of him. Once released, L.A. gladly stuck his dick in her mouth. He tasted like the richest toffee.

"I want you to fuck my mouth," she whimpered.

Always one to please, L.A. grabbed the back of her head and fucked her mouth like it was her pussy. He loved the sight of his ten inch, brown cock sliding in and out her wet mouth.

"Ooooooh." Chyna moaned as she deep-throated his dick.

"Yeah, just like that. Yeah, yeah; deep," L.A. instructed.

"Ahhhhhh! I love sucking your dick!" Chyna flicked her tongue across the tip.

L.A. could watch Chyna devour his penis for hours but he wanted to fuck. He wanted to feel every inch of her.

"Turn around." He lifted her up and flipped her over onto her stomach.

Chyna squealed with delight. Her round, juicy ass was hiked up in the air. His long python slapped up against her ass cheeks. Chyna gazed at him through the mirror. If she allowed herself, she could really fall for him. L.A. looked back at her as he placed on a condom. He was about to fuck her so long and hard she'd feel his dick all the way up in her cervix. Chyna parted her legs in anticipation of receiving him. L.A. ran his hand across her back as he teased her clit with the tip of his dick.

"L.A., fuck me." Chyna demanded unable to take the torture.

L.A. grinned at her. He was in no rush. He planned on fucking her all night. Slowly, he slid his hard, throbbing dick inside her wet pussy. The walls of her vagina felt so warm against his cock. Chyna gripped the sides of the sink and held on tight. She couldn't take her eyes off him. She'd never been so turned on in her life.

"Mmmmmmmmm," she shrilled as he stroked her middle.

"Ahhhhh! Ahhh, yeah!" He groaned fully aroused.

Chyna's pussy was the best. L.A. grabbed the bottle of Ace and poured some more of it down her back. He watched as the champagne slid between the crack of her ass and landed on his shaft.

"Yes! Just like that!" She panted unable to control herself. "That's it. You're hitting my spot!"

Grinding his hips, L.A. wet his fingers then reached around and played with her clit. Chyna really lost her mind then.

"L.A., fuck; I can't take! It feels so good! Yeah, ah yeah! Make me cum!"

By sunrise Chyna had cum so many times her body became numb. L.A. fucked her from the bathroom, to the chaise lounge, all the way to her bed. She'd been placed in every erotic position known to man. Ironically, she liked missionary with him the most. His dick seemed to hit her spine with every stroke. The connection they had was on a spiritual level.

Fucking L.A. felt so good it hurt. She couldn't get enough of him. It was like she'd taken her first hit of crack and become addicted. She thought sex with Carlos was amazing but L.A. took her to another galaxy. He made her squirt. Chyna didn't even know she could. She thought that was some mythical shit that only pornstars could do.

Famished, after fucking each other's brains out, they both showered and headed to Uncle Bill's for breakfast. Uncle Bill's was a South City staple. Chyna sat across from him in a tiny booth and tried not to remember the last time she was in a booth. She and L.A. placed their orders. Twenty minutes went by before their food came. L.A. reached across the table, took her hand and bowed his head.

"Lord, thank you for my health and this food. Let it be nourishing to my body and thank you for this beautiful, smart, sexy woman I get to share this meal with. Hopefully, she'll stop playin' around with my heart and give me a chance. In Jesus' name I pray, amen."

Chyna smiled and lifted her head. The only other time she had a man thank God for her was when Carlos did. Chyna hated to think about him while she sat across from L.A. but it was hard not to. She knew the act they'd committed was scandalous and unforgiveable. But she wasn't Carlos' girl. She was free to sleep with whomever she pleased. She didn't regret sleeping with L.A. at all. The long stroke he gave her was exactly what she needed and he was nice to look at.

"Amen," she repeated, then dug into her steak and eggs.

"So what was that all about?" He asked chewing his food.

"What was what all about?" Chyna asked perplexed.

"Last night. What was that about? What made you call me? You said you wasn't fuckin' with me, remember?"

"I know what I said," she laughed, cutting her steak. "You ain't gotta remind me. I hit you up... 'cause I wanted to see you," she smirked.

"Yeah, you wanted to see me a'ight. You wanted some dick."

"That too." She bugged up.

"You a trip."

"Last night was cute, though. It was a movie fa sho but let's just keep it at that. I don't want you to look too deep into it."

"Why? You still hung up on fake-ass Justin Bieber?" L.A. quizzed.

"You're ignorant," Chyna giggled. "No. The only man I'm hung up on is Jesus. Carlos and I are done."

"So what's up wit' me and you then?" L.A. asked seriously.

"Nothing." Chyna said without hesitation. "Not a damn thing."

"Chyna." He stared at her. "Stop frontin'. You like me. It's ok. You can admit it."

"You a'ight. You cool. I'm not looking for nothing serious though. So please do us both a favor and please do not catch feelings for me. That's the last thing I need right now 'cause I'm all over the place. I don't wanna lead you on and end up hurting you."

"You think I'm worried about you hurting me?" L.A. furrowed his brows. "Chyna, before you know it, you gon' end up fallin' in love with me." He said confidently.

"I'D RATHER YOU CHOSE ME EVERY DAY." – JAMES

BLAKE, "CHOOSE ME"

CHAPTER SIXTEEN

That Monday, Chyna brought in groceries from the grocery store. India would be home in a few hours. She wanted to make sure dinner was ready before she got there. It was cold as fuck outside and about to snow. St. Louis was in store for 4 to 6 inches of snow, heavy rain and sleet. Chyna couldn't wait to get into the house and warm up but she had more bags to bring in. The cab driver had already pulled off and she was left alone to bring in the bags herself.

On her third trip she went back outside to find Carlos standing in her doorway. Surprised to see him, she jumped back and clenched her chest. It seemed like he popped up out of nowhere. Carlos was the last person on earth she expected or wanted to see.

"Hi." He spoke trying to gage her reaction.

Chyna just stood there and stared at him.

"You need any help?" He asked.

"What are you doing here?" She finally questioned. "You know what?" She stopped him before he could speak. "It don't even matter. I need for you to go. My daughter will be home soon." She reached down to pick up her bags.

"Chyna, let me talk to you." He tried to take her hand.

"No!" She snatched her arm away. "I'm not dealing with this shit with you today. I told you to leave me alone. Have you figured out what you want to do?"

"That's why I'm here," he urged.

"Well, I don't care. I don't wanna hear shit you got to say." She picked up a few grocery bags. "Go home to Bellamy and leave me the fuck alone." She turned and tried to walk away.

"Nah, fuck that!" Carlos yanked her back and held her by the arms. "I'm not gon' let you run away! You gon' fuckin' listen!" He shook her profusely.

Shaken up, Chyna stood silent.

"I love you." He tried to make her understand.

Chyna heard the words he was saying but wasn't feeling shit he had to say.

"I don't wanna be with her. I want to be with you."

"Sorry to burst your bubble but I don't want you." She said evenly.

"C'mon, Chyna, stop with the games. You know you love me."

Chyna did love him. This was true but the taste of L.A.'s tongue still lingered on her lips. They'd had a wonderful weekend together. Loving Carlos just wasn't enough anymore.

"I don't care! Me and you are done. It's a wrap! You shouldn't have to think about whether or not you wanna be with me. I ain't no fuckin' afterthought, nigga!" She pushed him away, dropping her bags.

"Watch your fuckin' mouth," he warned.

"Fuck you! Leave... me... alone. You are killing me." She broke down. "Can't you see that? Loving someone shouldn't be this hard. You're no good for me and I'm no good for you."

"You're the best thing that's ever happened to me." He grabbed her and held her tight. "You're my baby. I can't see me being with anybody but you. You just have to trust and believe that I got you. I swear to God, I'm not gon' let you down."

"I don't have to do shit but stay black, die and pay my taxes. You know how stupid I look going back-and-forth with you? Just do me a favor," she pleaded, placing her hand in the praying position. "Forget I ever existed. Let's just act like none of this ever happened. You go your way and I'll go mine."

"I'm not fuckin' doing that."

"If you can't do it, I'll do it for you. Give me your phone." She held out her hand.

"Why?"

"Just give me your phone."

Carlos pulled his phone from his pocket and handed it to her.

"What are you doing?" He asked unsure of what her next move was gonna be.

"I'm about to erase my number from your phone so you won't ever have to think about callin' me again. What's your password?" She looked up at him.

"This is stupid." Carlos said pissed.

"Give me your password!" Chyna fumed.

"Eight, twenty-one, eighty-one." He huffed.

Chyna's arm dropped to her side. She hadn't expected for her birthday to be his password. Every time she thought she was out, he found a way to pull her back in again.

"My God." She groaned, rolling her eyes to the sky. "Why do you do this to me?" Tears slipped from the corner of her eyes.

She needed to get rid of Carlos and walk away from him for good. If they didn't part ways now, one of them was going to kill the other.

"I didn't mean to make you upset." He wiped her tears away. "That's the last thing I ever wanted to do." He kissed her eyelids, cheeks and lips.

"I love you," he whispered softly. "I love you."

Chyna opened her eyes. Her lips trembled from the tears she cried and the freezing cold weather. She wanted to run away but Carlos had her cornered. She couldn't walk away if she tried. His body heat encompassed her. He'd unbuttoned her coat and started massaging her breasts.

"I can't keep doing this with you," she cried as their lips met. "I can't let you hold me down. You can't just say you love me today. You have to choose me every day."

"I promise, I will." Carlos pulled down her leggings and gripped her ass.

"What the fuck were you thinkin'?" Brooke scolded Chyna over the phone.

"I don't know! I wasn't thinkin'. I got caught in the moment." Chyna answered scurrying back to the office with two trays of coffee in hand.

"You have taken hoing to an all new level. How you gon' fuck L.A. and Carlos a day apart from each other? Ain't yo' pussy sore? I bet you yo' pussy look like the bear from The Revenant," Brooke joked. "Bitch, you need to put that pussy on retirement. And please tell me you used a condom."

"I did with L.A." Chyna pressed the up button on the elevator.

"So are you and Carlos together? Like, what's going on?"

"I don't know," Chyna sighed. "I guess we're together. He said he wants to be with me but he said the same thing a week ago then we got into it. Girl, this whole thing is just one big-ass mess. I love Carlos but now I'm low-key feeling L.A. too."

"Nigga, you ain't Bella and this for damn sure ain't Twilight. You better choose and g'on with your life," Brooke advised. "Personally, I'm team L.A. He's a winner."

"But he's cool with Carlos, Brooke. I can't do that."

"Why not? You already fucked him!" Brooke shrilled. "You might as well be with him and stop bullshittin'. Friend, you can't keep on playing hard to get with a man that's hard to get. You better lock that nigga down before another bitch do."

"You're right." Chyna boarded the elevator. "But how can I try to build something new with L.A. when my heart is still with Carlos? No matter how hard I try, I can't push my feelings for him away. I think, if given the chance, we can really make it work."

"You gotta do what's best for you. Just be smart, friend. Don't let no cracker play you," Brooke warned, sternly.

"I won't," Chyna cracked up laughing. "But look, I gotta go. I'll call you later." She got off on her floor.

"A'ight and put that pussy up!" Brooke shouted before she hung up.

Chyna snickered and ended the call. The whole writing staff was waiting on her to return with their Starbucks orders. Chyna didn't realize until she got all the way to Starbucks and stood in line that she'd left the list with everyone's order on her desk. She couldn't risk going back and getting reamed out by Felicia so she tried to remember everyone's order off the top of her head.

She had ten cups of coffee to get, including Felicia's, so she prayed that she got them all right. Chyna handed the cups to all of the writing staff. By the disgruntled looks on their faces, she quickly realized she'd gotten them all wrong. Felicia was especially pissed because she'd specifically asked for no milk because she was lactose intolerant but Chyna got it anyway.

To make matters worse, it wasn't Chyna's only mishap of the day. She'd screwed up the printer, transferred several calls to the wrong person and showed up 20 minutes late. Her mind was all over the place. She couldn't focus. All she could think about was her trysts with L.A. and Carlos. She never imagined she'd be hung up on two men at the same time.

What she and L.A. had was fairly new. She didn't know what she wanted from him if anything at all. They had mad chemistry. The sex was life-altering. He seemed to really adore her and want to get to know more about her. She found herself wanting to go beyond the surface with him as well but was afraid of letting Carlos go.

If she truly gave L.A. a chance that would mean she'd have to close the door on her romance with Carlos. Chyna wasn't ready to do that quite yet. They were finally starting to get somewhere. She couldn't give up on him now. She also couldn't keep obsessing over her love triangle. It was doing nothing but getting her in trouble. Her chaotic love life not only mind fucked her but got her sent home early.

Felicia saw that she wasn't focused and angrily told her to go home and try again the next day. Chyna begged to stay. She promised that there wouldn't be any more mistakes but Felicia wasn't trying to hear her plea. By 2:30pm, Chyna solemnly strolled up her walkway. Disappointed wasn't the word to describe how she felt about herself. She couldn't let her man troubles fuck up her opportunity.

She had to get it together and fast. A clear and concise decision had to be made before she ruined everything she'd worked so hard for. Pulling out her key, Chyna went to unlock the door when she found it already open.

"India!" She panicked.

"Mom!" India raced down the steps.

"Why is the door wide open?" Chyna's heart raced. "Are you okay?"

"Come here. You have to see this!" India pulled her mom up the steps.

Chyna walked into the kitchen/living and dining room area and found it filled from wall-to-wall with flowers. There were bouquets of pink roses and tulips. Chyna had never seen a sight so beautiful. The second floor of her house had been turned into a pink botanical garden. The flowers instantly lifted her spirits.

"The delivery man just dropped all of these off." India said in awe.

Chyna placed her purse down, mesmerized.

"He was telling the truth," she whispered to herself, overjoyed.

Carlos was really putting forth the effort to prove he was serious about making them official. With her was where he wanted to be. Chyna searched for a card to further confirm that the flowers were from him.

"Did they come with a note?" She asked India.

"Just this one." India handed it to her.

Chyna giddily opened the envelope and found a lovely handwritten note that simply said:

Thinkin' about you always.

L.A.

Her heart sank a little when she realized the flowers weren't from Carlos but blossomed when she saw how much L.A. cared for her. It was apparent he wasn't going to let up on pursuing her. She liked that he made her a priority.

"Who are they from?" India died to know.

"A really good friend of mine," Chyna reddened, holding the note close to her chest. "Give me a minute so I can call and say thank you." She asked India kindly.

"I'ma find out who those flowers are from," India promised. "Whoever sent them to you is pretty dope, Mom." She clarified on the way to her room.

Chyna couldn't argue with a thing she said. L.A. was a pretty dope individual. If he kept it up he might just find a permanent place in her heart. Chyna pulled her phone out her purse and dialed his number. As the phone rang she walked around the room touching and smelling the striking flowers.

"What's up, love?" His deep voice boomed through the phone.

"You. Thanks for the flowers." Chyna smiled, shyly.

"It's nothing. I'm happy you like them. What you up to?"

"About to take my clothes off and go to bed. I had a rough day."

"Nah, let me take you out."

"I would but I'm just not in the mood today. I hope you understand." She prayed he did.

"How about this," L.A. negotiated unwilling to take no for an answer. "How about instead of going out, we stay in? I'll bring everything to you."

Chyna sighed heavily. She wanted to protest. After what had happened over the weekend, she needed to stay as far away from L.A. as possible. But as she looked around the room at the thoughtful gesture he'd made, there was no way she could say no.

"TELL ME WHAT WE'RE DOING, BABE." - JANE HANDCOCK,

"LA NIGGA"

CHAPTER SEVENTEEN

Nowhere near in the mood to try to be cute, Chyna took a shower, removed her makeup, threw on a ratty, old, tank top and jeans. If L.A. liked her as much as he claimed he did, then he would have no problem with her looking a hot mess. Chyna was tired of trying to impress niggas anyway. It was time for her to be her 100% authentic self. She was over trying to prove how dope of a woman she was.

She knew she'd make some man a wonderful wife one day. She just kept giving her heart to fuckboys that didn't deserve the time of day. It was high time a man proved his worth to her. Until then, she was going to piece together the broken fragments of her life and try to make sense of it all. Chyna needed the space, opportunity and time to do so. She desperately needed her life to go from EDM to chop and screwed. Chyna couldn't do nothing but crack up laughing when L.A. showed up on her doorstep with bags of Popeyes chicken.

"How did you know Popeyes was my favorite," she gushed.

"A little birdie told me," he winked his eye causing her to melt.

"You talked to Brooke?" Chyna questioned, squinting her eyes.

"Who?" L.A. asked unaware of who Brooke was. "Nah, I stalked your Facebook." He showed off his boyish grin.

"No you ain't doing research on me." Chyna playfully pushed him in the arm.

"I read two of your books too." He pulled the food out of the bags.

Chyna stood speechless for a second. No man, not even Tyreik, had ever sat down and read her books.

"Which ones?" She asked skeptical.

"Torn and Paper Heart. You a beast with the pen, love." He gave her a quick peck on the cheek.

Even though Chyna was dressed down with no makeup, he was still very attracted to her. She could do no wrong in his eyes. Chyna turned beet red and tried to conceal her smile. She treasured when he called her love.

"Thank you."

"I bought enough for me, you and your daughter; is that okay?" L.A. inquired washing his hands.

Chyna blinked her eyes several times. The fact that he'd taken out the time to think about India meant the world to her.

"Yes, of course." She tried her best to contain her elation. "India! Come upstairs! It's time to eat!"

India placed her game on pause and came into the kitchen.

"India, meet my good friend, L.A. L.A, this is my fabulous daughter, India." Chyna wrapped her arm around her daughter's shoulder.

"It's a pleasure to meet you." L.A. extended his hand.

"Hi," India shook his hand and tried not to faint. "Mom, you didn't tell me that L.A was your friend? Do you know who he is? He's a two-time champ and MVP!"

"As you can see, my daughter's a sports fan," Chyna smirked.

"That's hella cool. It's rare to see a girl into sports." L.A. responded. "Has anyone ever told you how much you look like your mother?"

"All the time," India rolled her eyes, embarrassed.

"Well look, I bought us all some Popeyes since it's your mom's favorite."

"Mine too," India added.

"Looks like I made the right choice then. Let's dig in." He made Chyna and India a plate.

"Mom, can I eat in my room?"

"Yeah but you bet not waste anything," Chyna cautioned.

"Mom," India huffed. "I'm 15. I'm pretty sure I can play the game and eat at the same time without wasting anything."

"What you playin'?" L.A. quizzed.

He was an avid gamer himself.

"Call of Duty: Advanced Warfare."

"That's my shit. You mind if I play wit' you?"

"Can he, Mom?" India said thrilled.

She hardly ever got to play her game with anyone.

"Yeah, we'll all play." Chyna said down for a night of chicken, biscuits and fun.

For almost two hours they all sat in India's room killing army men and eating spicy chicken wings. There was non-stop laughter and smack talking. Chyna enjoyed every second of it. She hadn't seen India so alive. It was as if she came to life. She and L.A. hit it off instantaneously. They were like long-lost buddies.

Chyna never imagined he would be so good with kids, let alone a teenage girl. Throughout the night, Chyna found herself in complete adoration of L.A. He was proving himself to be more than the arrogant, rich boy, millionaire she thought he was. He was actually very kind, charming, lively, family-orientated and romantic. The playboy, backstabber had completely vanished.

The man he'd revealed himself to be was far less abrasive and more appealing. Without being overly dramatic or deliberate, he touched places in her heart that had never been tapped into. For the first time in her life, she felt like she had a family. Chyna hated to think that way. It was way too soon to be having those kind of thoughts. L.A. wasn't even her man. He wasn't India's father but to see the smile he put on her face made Chyna wish that he was.

Being in a family setting made Chyna realize how much she craved the stability. She was tired of fucking with one dude after another. She wanted something more than a one-night stand or meaningless sex. She wanted someone that despite her flaws, mistakes or insecurities, would choose to love her every day.

She'd had her ups and downs when it came to love. Looking back on her life, Chyna wasn't sure if she had ever really been in love before. She'd been in toxic relationships but never experienced true love. L.A. made her feel like it could be a possibility. Maybe Cupid had finally hit a bull's-eye.

When it was time for India to get ready for bed she and L.A. said their goodbyes. L.A. vowed to return to play the game with her again if Chyna allowed. Back in the kitchen he helped her wash the dishes. Chyna told him she could do it alone but he insisted on drying them for her. Halfway through, her drain started to act up. L.A., being the hands-on man he was, didn't hesitate to jump in and see what the problem was.

"Step back". He scooted Chyna out of the way and tinkered with the switch.

When that didn't work, he went under the sink and fiddled with a few things.

"Now see if it works," he instructed.

Chyna flipped the switch and it worked perfectly. *This nigga handy too,* she thought as he rose to his feet and dusted off his shirt. Once the dishes were clean and dried, L.A. grabbed his coat to leave. Chyna didn't want him to leave but kept her mouth shut. She didn't want to come across thirsty.

She'd warned L.A. not to fall for her but it seemed like the tables were being turned. As Chyna walked him to his car and the stars twinkled from above, she found herself wanting to beg for him to stay. L.A. leaned his back against the driver side door of his white Range Rover. He'd had an amazing day with Chyna.

It was the most fun he had in a while. She was the truth. He knew that she was a good girl 'cause he was a good dude. Put the two of them together and they could change the world. L.A. loved everything about her. He loved her hair, the way she smiled. He appreciated her godly figure. She was the coolest. She was a great mom, sassy, unapologetic and hardworking.

To him, she was the next best thing on earth. He loved being on top of her while she looked into his eyes. He tried to hide how he felt for her but it was futile. All of the pieces of his heart he wanted to give to her. L.A. wanted her to be his lady. He wanted to go to sleep with her in his arms and wake up to her pretty face. She was meant to be his wife. He was just waiting on her to realize that she was wifey material.

"Come here." He pulled her into him by the belt loop of her jeans.

Chyna stepped up and stood in-between his firm legs. A cool breeze swept over them as she gazed into his intense eyes.

"Tell me something about you that nobody else knows." He asked sincerely.

"Like what?" Chyna replied guarded.

"I wanna know more about you. Not just that you're a single mother but what you dream and hope for."

At that moment, Chyna decided to forgo being hard. She was sick of pretending like love was a game she could win. She was failing miserably. Once again, it had snuck up on her and taken over.

"I wanna be happy," she confessed, choking up on her words.

"I can make you happy," he professed kissing her fervently.

Chyna closed her eyes and reveled in his sweet kisses. L.A. tasted like midnight. He tasted like wine. She could see them being together forever. She couldn't act like he wasn't in her daydreams. The feelings she had for him was wearing on her heart. Their friendship had turned to love. She couldn't front anymore. It was time to let her guard down. She was catching feelings for him. It dawned on her, as he wrapped her up in his embrace, that she truly cared about L.A.

She genuinely felt bad for sleeping with him and Carlos in the same weekend. She never wanted him to find out in fear of losing him for good. She could no longer teeter between the two. She had to make a choice.

"I CALL AND YOU PRESS IGNORE." –ELLE MAI, "I WISH"

CHAPTER EIGHTEEN

Raindrops the size of lemon drops tapped against the windowpane. Bellamy gazed out upon the skyline somberly. There she was spending another night at home alone. Carlos was supposed to have been home hours ago. Yet he still hadn't walked through the door or bothered to call. Since her ultimatum, things between them had gone from bad to worse. They barely talked and when they did, their conversations seemed forced.

Sex had become a chore. He acted like he barely wanted to touch her. Bellamy was doing all she could to look past his lies and infidelity but with each day it became increasingly hard. She couldn't continue to stand by and be disrespected by someone she loved. She couldn't go on living like a ghost in her own home. If Carlos loved her so much, he had a lousy way of showing it.

It was abundantly clear that the reason he wasn't home was because he was with his mistress. Bellamy took a pull off the cigarette in her manicured hand and envisioned him kissing and hugging Chyna the way he used to kiss and hug her. She never imagined that another chick would be getting the love that was supposed to be on reserve for her. It wasn't fair. It wasn't fair that Chyna got the best parts of him while she had to settle for his scraps.

It wasn't fair that Bellamy had been reduced to smoking cigarettes. This wasn't her life. She was over being blindly in love with a man that treated her feelings like a casual fling. She couldn't take one more day of being stabbed in the chest by his arrogant-ass behavior. She worked too damn hard during the day to be this stressed out at night.

Bellamy was supposed to be in bed asleep hours ago but there was no way she could rest until he was home. If he kept this shit up, she had to figure out a way to say goodbye. It would be extremely hard to go on without him but her pride couldn't take the constant beating. Carlos was either going to grow up or get left behind. There was no gray area anymore.

Bellamy was starting to see things much clearer now. Her parents didn't raise no fool and she wasn't about to start playing the part now. Envisioning herself becoming fuckboy free, she scowled as she heard Carlos walk across the threshold at midnight. She immediately spun around on her heels to face him. The lips of her pussy ached as he walked in.

She hated that she still lusted after him. That was Carlos' problem. He knew he was fine. A man that was aware of his good looks was always a problem. Carlos took his brown, leather jacket and hat off. He placed them on the coatrack and swept his hair from out of his face. The olive green hoodie, white, extended tee, ripped jeans and butter-colored Tims he donned was street style at its finest.

If he wasn't so fine, Bellamy would've been found the strength to leave him a long time ago. But no, here she was filling her lungs up with nicotine just to spite him. Carlos licked his bottom lip and looked at her. Bellamy was still dressed in her work clothes. Her eyes were bloodshot red from crying. Mascara was smudged all over her face. She was a wreck.

"What's wrong with you and since when you start smoking cancer sticks?" He rubbed his hands together to warm up.

Carlos hated the smell of cigarette smoke, especially in his house. It would take days to get the foul stench out.

"You... you're my problem. I know you were with that bitch." Bellamy took another long drag from the cigarette then exhaled it up into the air.

"What?" Carlos eyed her with contempt.

"You heard me. Y'all have fun tonight? What did you do? Did you take her to dinner or a movie? You know, basic hoes like basic things."

"What the fuck are you talkin' about?" Carlos shot, already over her line of questioning. "I was at the restaurant with Knight. Me, him and some of the cooks stayed late and had a couple of drinks," he said truthfully.

"Yeah, sure you did," Bellamy spat not believing a word that came out of his mouth. "I guess you must really take me for a fool."

"I'm tellin' you the truth. You wanna call him since you don't believe me?" He tried to hand her his phone.

"So you can make me look crazy to all of our friends? I don't think so." She slapped his hand away.

"You really need to seek help 'cause you're fuckin' crazy." Carlos scoffed heading towards the refrigerator.

"If I'm crazy it's because you made me this way! You did this to me!" Bellamy shouted, pointing her finger at him. "It's funny 'cause I was so sure. I thought I could keep you somehow. I didn't care how I did it. I was determined to have you. I never thought you'd leave me but... now I've lost. I must admit, I expected more of a—"

"A fight?" Carlos finished her sentence. "Why? I don't wanna fight with you. I'm trying to get over you."

Tears formed in Bellamy's eyes and clouded her vision. His words were like knives to her chest. If Carlos was trying to kill her, he was succeeding.

"What did I ever do to you? All I ever did was try to love you. I tried to give you everything you ever wanted. We were supposed to be together until the day we died."

Carlos felt like a complete asshole for making her feel this way. At one point he did see himself being with her until they were gray and old but people grow and things change.

"Well, you're getting your wish now. 'Cause I don't wanna be with you anymore. It's over and since it's over... I suppose I should wish you two happiness but I don't! I hope you're fuckin' miserable!" Bellamy spat heatedly.

"Yeah, that's more like you. I was wondering when the real Bellamy was gon' come out," Carlos scoffed not surprised by her venomous well wishes.

"I'm not doing this wit' you tonight. I'm getting the fuck up out of here." He changed directions and headed to their bedroom.

He was going to pack a bag and get a hotel room for the night.

"You ain't going nowhere!" Bellamy put the cigarette out on the back of the couch and ran behind him. "I made you, muthafucka! Now you wanna treat me like I was the corny muthafucka from the projects!"

"What you say?" Carlos stopped dead in his tracks and turned around.

"Yeah, I said it. You were a corny, lame-ass muthafucka! Nobody wanted you. Look at the life you have now because of me. Now you wanna leave me for her? That raggedy, ghetto bitch!" Bellamy cried so hard her head began to hurt.

"You really think that's how this is gonna go down? You are mine!" Her lips quivered.

Before Carlos could respond, his phone started to ring. Carlos pulled his phone from his pocket. He and Bellamy both looked down at the screen. It was Chyna.

"Oh, there goes your bitch now! Answer the phone!" She placed her hand on her hip. "Go ahead. Answer it!" She demanded.

Carlos clenched his jaw. He wanted to answer but now was not the right time so he let the phone ring.

"Oh, you're not gonna answer? You can put her on speaker phone. We can both talk to her," Bellamy mocked.

"You fuckin' crazy, yo. Get the fuck outta here with that dumb shit." Carlos resumed walking towards the bedroom.

"Oh, you mad 'cause I'm tellin' the truth? The truth hurts don't it, bitch?" Bellamy forcefully mushed him in the back of his head causing his head to jerk forward.

Unable to control his rage, Carlos spun around, grabbed her by the arms and swung her down onto the floor.

"What I tell you about puttin' your hands on me? You like for me to get aggressive wit' you!" He shook her. "You like for me to put my hands on you? You like for me to act outside of myself! Quit actin' so fuckin' stupid!"

"It's the only way I can get your attention!" Bellamy wept. "Why don't you love me anymore?" She sobbed as he held her hands firmly above her head.

"'Cause you think you're better than me! You treat me like a little-ass boy. I'm not Dash! I'm not your fuckin' child! I'm a grown-ass man, Bellamy. I can do whatever the fuck I wanna do! You don't run me. I told you several times that I needed space but you ain't wanna do that. So don't cry now. I tried to spare your feelings."

"Don't try to turn this shit around on me like I'm the problem. You're the one that's cheating on me! And how dare you speak my son's name right now!" She fought for him to get off of her to no avail.

Carlos held her down, unwilling to get up when his phone rang again. A few blocks away, Chyna held her phone up to her ear pacing back-and-forth. She needed to talk to Carlos ASAP. She needed a firm yes or no on if they were going to be together or not. Three rings into the call, she was sent to voicemail.

"Oh no the fuck he didn't." She stared at the phone flabbergasted. "He's with that bitch." Chyna's body grew tense.

Since he wouldn't answer her calls, she decided to text him.

<Messages Carlos Details

I need to talk to u

Carlos read the text and placed his phone face down on the floor beside him. Chyna would have to wait.

"Get off of me! Go talk to your whore!" Bellamy kicked and screamed.

"I'm not gettin' up till you act like you got some fuckin' sense."

"I hate you!" Bellamy's chest heaved up-and-down. "On everything I love. I fucking hate you. Look at what you've done to me. I don't even know who I am anymore. If Dash was here none of this would be happening right now."

Seeing the agony on her face tore Carlos up inside. He understood the turmoil she felt. It was like they were mourning the death of their baby boy all over again. This time, it was worse because their relationship was dying as well.

Chyna waited a few minutes then texted him once more. Carlos' phone was always near him. There was no excuse for him not to respond to her unless he was occupied with another bitch.

<Messages   Carlos   Details

HELLO?

I KNOW U SEE ME CALLIN' U!!!

R U WITH HER RIGHT NOW?

Carlos let go of Bellamy's hands and wiped her tears away. It fucked him up to see her cry. The death of their baby boy would always tug on both of their heartstrings.

"I can't do this. Just leave me alone if you don't wanna be with me anymore," she pleaded.

"Shhhh," Carlos kissed her tenderly. "Stop." He parted her lips with his.

Their tongues intertwined and danced around each other passionately. What happened next came as natural as the air they breathed. Carlos' hands roamed up her shirt and cupped her breasts. He had no business making love to her but it was what they both needed.

He wasn't ready to leave her behind. Bellamy would always have a special place in his heart. She was his first love, his ex-wife. The way he loved her should've been a sin. And yes, he'd told Chyna that she would be the one he chose but at that moment the hard-on inside his jeans needed a release.

Bellamy lay under Carlos. Each kiss he placed on her skin felt like bullet wounds. She wanted to protest as he entered her slit but she couldn't find the words. She'd promised herself that things wouldn't end like this. Temporary love making wouldn't heal the layers of scars he'd created. She knew he was only placating her to ease his own guilt. But there was something about him she just couldn't erase.

Chyna sat before her bed on the hardwood floor feeling like a complete idiot. Tears scorched her cheeks. She'd let him do it to her again. Once again Carlos' actions didn't match his words. No more. Chyna was done. Carlos was nothing but Tyreik dressed up in a prettier package.

She'd fallen for a clone of him. The only difference between the two men was that Carlos hadn't physically put his hands on her. The psychological abuse he put her through was far worse. Bruises would heal but mental abuse left you scarred for life. Chyna thought she had escaped the madness but nothing had changed.

The tears that fell from her eyes still felt the same. Carlos claimed to love her but she still sat alone while he spent his time with another woman. Once again, Chyna was someone's second choice. She hadn't learned her lesson yet. Until she did she would keep on dating men like Carlos and Tyreik. It was high time she realized that she was good enough to be loved wholeheartedly.

Love wasn't one big constant disappointment after another. Love shouldn't make you feel less than what you are. Chyna was done for good. As she sat in a puddle of her own tears, she made the conscious decision to stop the cycle of abuse. She could no longer blame Carlos for treating her the way he did. She allowed him to do it. There would be no more falling for his lies. Her self-worth and pride was far more important than having Carlos around.

What made him think she didn't want a man she could call her own? She wasn't going to wait on him forever. She didn't want to be unhappy. Chyna couldn't have another sleepless night wondering if Carlos wanted her or not. She could do bad on her own.

The longer she dealt with him she was only hurting herself. In the end, he was the one winning anyway. He had two women pining after him. Well, Chyna was getting off the bus. She was over him treating her heart like a play toy. She refused to let him destroy her like Tyreik had nearly done. Bellamy could have his ass.

As far as Chyna was concerned, he could suck her balls. She didn't give a fuck. She was giving up. Nothing else had to be said after that night; she was blocking him out of her life for good. Chyna went to her contacts and blocked his number. She didn't need him to make a choice. She was strong enough to do it on her own. She was going to choose herself.

"I CAN'T PRETEND LIKE I DESERVE YOU AT ALL. IT'S LIKE YOU FELL FROM THE SKY." – COULTRAIN, "THE REINTRODUCTION"

CHAPTER NINETEEN

Thanksgiving, Christmas and New Year's had come and gone. Chyna had a glorious holiday season with the people she loved. She showered India with gifts and in turn was showered with gifts from L.A. He got her and India everything their hearts desired. If Chyna let him, he would spoil the both of them to death.

Now that the holiday season was over, Martin Luther King Day was fast approaching. Chyna had finally finished her spec. She was extremely proud of the episode she'd written. She'd put her heart and soul into it. She put it all out on the table. Removing the drama of having Carlos in her life was a big help. With him gone, she was able to concentrate on the positive things in her life.

He'd tried coming by to talk but Chyna didn't answer the door. She didn't have anything for him. She was moving on with her life and leaving the bullshit behind. She even had the Cartier bracelets he'd bought her unlocked. She didn't want a reminder of him anywhere on her body.

She and L.A. were growing extremely close. It was the middle of the NBA season, so when he wasn't on the road, they spent every waking moment together. When they were apart, he made sure to FaceTime Chyna every day. She treasured his devotion to her.

He made her feel special. She prayed that she could give him the same love and devotion in return. She never wanted to disappoint or hurt him. L.A. deserved the best. He took his time with her. He always took the time to make sure she was comfortable. Chyna couldn't have asked for a better man. Because of him, she knew what the real was. The shit she had with Tyreik and Carlos was fake and superficial. There would be no turning back now that she'd had a taste of real, pure love.

Chyna nervously walked to Felicia's office with her spec in hand. She prayed she liked it. She was done with being an errand girl. She was thankful for the opportunity but Chyna was ready to put in work. Taking a deep breath, she lightly tapped on the door and turned the knob.

Chyna stepped in and quickly jumped back. Felicia was on top of her desk with her back to the door. Her legs were spread open and her head was cocked back. Soft moans of gratification escaped from her lips as Warren gave her head.

"Oh my God!" Chyna screeched, mortified.

Frightened, Felicia sat up straight and clasped her legs closed.

"Chyna, what the hell are you doing in my office?" She yelled as Warren struggled to get off his knees.

Felicia had his head gripped between her thighs.

"I am so sorry." Chyna shielded her eyes with her spec and backed out of the room.

"Close the door behind you!"

"Okay-okay-okay." Chyna frantically pulled the door shut.

A nervous wreck, she stood outside the door fanning herself. Seeing Felicia receiving head from the president of HBO was the last thing she ever wanted to see. *Why me, Lord?* She tried to compose herself. Several minutes later, Felicia's door opened and Warren walked out.

"Have a good day." He cleared his throat while straightening his tie.

"You too, sir." Chyna replied, wanting to shrivel up and die.

"Chyna! Get in here now!" Felicia called from her desk.

Chyna hung her head and reentered the room.

"Have a seat," Felicia ordered.

"Felicia, I am so sorry. I had no idea you weren't alone," Chyna said sorrowfully.

"I wasn't. Next time wait until I tell you to come in," she instructed.

"Yes, ma'am."

"What is it that you need?" Felicia carried on as if nothing happened.

"Ummmm," Chyna's mind went blank for a second.

She was never good at playing the game of pretend. The visual of Warren eating Felicia's coochie like it was his last supper still lingered in her brain. She'd never be able to look at her the same.

"I came to give you this." Chyna finally came to and handed her the spec.

"You finally finished?" Felicia gave a slight smile.

"Yes, and I worked really hard on it."

"I hope so. Your career in The Writers' Room depends on it. I'll let you know what I think when I'm done." Felicia gave her a look that said now it's time for you to go.

"Thank you and again I'm sorry," Chyna apologized, scurrying out of the office.

Wait till I tell Brooke and Asia this!

It was time to turn up and HG Dance Club was the perfect place to do it. HG was St. Louis' premier nightlife destination. Performers from all over the world performed there. Upon entry, partygoers were surrounded by style and luxury. Everything on the inside was cocaine white. Neon strobe lights lit up the place.

Drinks were being passed. Bodies were pressed up against one another. Chyna stood in the midst of it all with her friends dancing her butt off. Her hips just wouldn't stop grooving. She was having the time of her life. She had all of her best friends beside her. Asia was in town for the weekend. Chyna, Brooke, Asia and Delicious drank premium vodka, shook their asses and took videos for Snap Chat.

Chyna was in the zone. She hadn't felt this alive in a long while. Being drama free was the way to be. Chyna shined her Ty-Lite on her face and checked herself in her camera phone. Her natural, short curls framed her face. Her face was beat to capacity. Black, winged liner, Lily Lashes and reddish-orange lipstick was the focal point of her soft and sultry beat.

She rocked a brown, off-the-shoulder, sweet heart neckline, long sleeve, bodycon dress, Dsquared, jeweled, strappy heels and a jewel box-inspired Dolce & Gabbana purse. L.A. was on his way to the club to see her. She had to make sure she was still on point after dancing the night away. They hadn't seen each other in over a week. It would take everything in her not to pull her panties to the side and fuck him somewhere the lights were dim.

"You cute." Asia poked her in the side, playfully.

"Thanks," Chyna turned off her Ty-Lite.

"Where yo' boo at?"

"He's on the way," Chyna blushed.

She couldn't wait to see her baby. She missed him terribly. She hated whenever he was gone. Visions of him bending her over and taking her from behind while she watched through the bathroom mirror filled her mind.

"Look at you," Asia gushed, surprised by her friend's fondness of L.A. "You really like him, don't you?"

"I do," Chyna responded truthfully.

Her heart filled with so much admiration when she thought of L.A. She'd never been loved like this before. With him she felt full, high off life. When she looked into his eyes she saw nothing but love. He made her feel secure. Chyna's only fear was her fucking things up. She was prone to do dumb shit. With L.A., she didn't want to make any mistakes. Homeboy was a winner and she was willing to do anything to keep him. The respect she had for him was unparalleled. He was an upstanding man that demanded respect and didn't play any games.

Suddenly the crowd went wild. Everyone was losing their minds. Over the music, Chyna could hear girls screaming at the top of their lungs. She couldn't do anything but beam. The young bull had arrived. Chyna took pride in knowing he was coming to see her. L.A. and his boys cut through the crowd with security surrounding them.

He looked good as fuck. The heartbeat in her clit started thumping overtime. L.A. made her horny as hell. Couldn't none of the dudes in the club fuck with him.

His hair was freshly cut. Chyna couldn't wait to run her hands through his scruffy beard. His 6 foot 3 frame was the perfect hanger for the Mariner's baseball jersey, denim jeans and black and white, high-top Fendi sneakers he wore. A pair of gold, round frame shades covered his eyes. Three, thin, gold chains shined from his neck. The sleeve of tattoos on his arms danced under the club lights. The nigga was fine as fuck and he was all hers.

L.A. took over the club as soon as he walked in. All eyes were on him. A Cuban cigar hung from the corner of his lips. Hoes were eye-fuckin' him while dudes either showed love or hit him with the screw face. L.A. didn't give a fuck about none of that. He was there to see his baby. No other chick in the club had anything on her. She was perfect.

Chyna was of a different breed. Babygirl was the realest. Her attitude was real rude but necessary to handle a dude like him. She was the perfect piece of arm candy but L.A. wanted her to be more than that. He wanted her to be his wife. L.A. spotted Chyna standing in the center of the V.I.P. section looking like a black Miss America. The dress she wore clung to her hips and ass. Her caramel titties bounced every time she moved. She was summertime fine. He couldn't wait to get his hands on her. Chyna smiled from ear-to-ear as he approached.

"Hey, love." She wrapped her arms around his neck and pressed her titties against his chest.

"That's how we feelin' today?" He grinned, palming her plump ass.

"Mmm hmm," she smirked.

"Keep on playin'. I'ma stick this dick up in you."

"Promise," she flirted.

"Yep." He kissed her on the neck and allowed his hands to roam all over her body.

L.A. missed her sexy ta-tas and thighs. Chyna was his dream girl. She'd put up a fight but he'd arrested the coochie and her feelings got cuffed. She loved his dick game but his intelligence was really what captivated her. He and Chyna would sit up for hours and talk about everything from hip hop to racism in America.

"Let me introduce you to my friends." She called her friends over so they could get to know him.

After exchanging pleasantries, L.A., being the gentleman he was, had several bottles of Veuve Clicquot sent over to the table.

"Girl, I like him." Delicious looked L.A. up-and-down approvingly. "Nigga buying bottles and shit."

"I told you," Brooke chimed in. "She hardheaded. We could've been gettin' free drinks," she joked.

"I like him too," Asia announced. "But not because of the drinks. I like the way he makes you feel. Since he's gotten here you haven't stopped smiling."

"He's the best. I love him."

After the club, Chyna and L.A. headed back to his crib. She'd only been there a few times due to his hectic schedule. L.A. had several homes. He had homes in St. Louis, Los Angeles and Miami. His spot in St. Louis was in Architectural Digest. It was a 5 million dollar, three bedroom, four bathroom home. The traditional-style, two-story home featured bay windows, an airy living room with a large, painted, brick fireplace, spacious master bedroom that included a sitting area and a wooden patio made for backyard barbecues.

Chyna kicked off her heels and followed him into his state-of-the-art kitchen. She was starving. L.A.'s personal chef had food prepared for him on the stove. There was fried chicken, mac & cheese, collard greens and cornbread.

"That looks so good," Chyna salivated as he fixed them both a plate. "Big ups to Chef D! I can't believe you and Khaled have the same chef."

"Me either."

Chyna and L.A. said grace and began to eat.

"Man, this is so good." She savored every bite.

"Yeah, she did her thing." L.A. took a bite of collard greens.

"What you got planned for the rest of the weekend?" Chyna inquired.

"Fuckin' you." He eyed her lustfully.

"You are so fuckin' nasty," she giggled.

"You like it," L.A. winked his eye and parted her legs.

While eating his food he thumbed her clit.

"Stop. You're gettin' me wet," Chyna panted, trying not to cum all over his hand.

"That's the point," L.A. smirked as her phone rang. "Who in the hell callin' you this early in the morning?" He stopped playing with her pussy and furrowed his brows.

"I don't know," Chyna shrugged. "I don't even recognize the number."

"You think it might be India callin' from one of her friend's phone?" L.A. asked concerned.

"It might be. Let me see." Chyna answered, nervously. "Hello?"

"Hey," Carlos spoke deep into the phone.

"Who is this?"

"Now you don't know my voice?" Carlos asked, figuring she was trying to be funny.

Chyna rolled her eyes so hard she thought they were going to pop out.

"Why are you callin' me? No, don't call my phone no more. Lose my number." She hung up in his ear.

"Who was that?" L.A. asked seeing her frustration.

"Carlos." Chyna blocked the number from her phone.

"Why is he callin' you?"

"I have no idea. I blocked his number from my phone. I guess that's why he called from a number I didn't know."

"Y'all ain't been dealing with each other at all?" L.A. questioned unsure.

"No. I have not spoken to that man. I don't want anything to do with him."

"You sure about that?" L.A. quizzed.

"Absolutely," Chyna looked at him like he was crazy. "Carlos is so last season."

"Keep it that way. If you're done let it be done. Don't let me find out no different," L.A. ice grilled her.

"Jealousy is not cute on you," Chyna grinned, devilishly.

"Yeah a'ight, whatever." L.A. resumed eating.

"No seriously, you're so cute when you're jealous." She planted a soft kiss on his cheek. "Baby, you have nothing to worry about. All I want is you."

"Is that right?" L.A.'s dick grew hard.

"You know it." She lovingly kissed the side of his face.

"As soon as I'm finished eating, I'm fuckin' the shit outta you."

"We can get it crackin' right now," Chyna challenged.

"Nah, I need to fuel up first," L.A. laughed. "Damn." He placed his fork down. "I gotta go see my mom tomorrow," he remembered.

"You've barely told me anything about your parents."

"They cool. They've been married for over 20 years. My dad is real chill. He's my best friend. He's a good dude. My old bird, on the other hand, is a trip. Over the last couple of years, she kinda been treating my old dude bad. She be talkin' to him kind of reckless and shit."

"That's fucked up. Yo' daddy don't say nothin' back?"

"Not really. He's like me. He don't like all that arguing and fighting and shit. He just let her go off then he goes and does his own thing."

"That's sad," Chyna poked out her bottom lip.

"Yea... I love my mom. She just gotta chill."

"Well, I love you." Chyna hopped down from her seat and onto his lap.

L.A. examined her face and her words. There wasn't a part of him that doubted her. He wanted to tell her that he loved her first but fear of being rejected consumed him. To know that Chyna felt the same about him was the best gift he'd ever received. The love they shared was unwavering and real. He just prayed that Carlos was out of the picture. He didn't think that Chyna was checkin' for him anymore but L.A. knew Carlos well. He wasn't going to give up on her that easily. He was going to put up a fight.

"I told you, you was gon' fall in love with me." He scooped her up in his strong arms and carried her to his bedroom.

"What about the food?" Chyna giggled, holding onto his neck.

"Fuck that food. I'm about to make you scream my name."

"HOW COULD YOU EVER LOOK ME IN THE EYE AND TELL ME ALL YOUR GODDAMN LIES?" – ELLE MAI, "ONE DAY"

CHAPTER TWENTY

"Come on, love! Hurry up!" L.A. yelled from the second floor of Chyna's house.

"Yeah, Mom! Come on! We're going to miss the movie!" India added, anxiously.

"Oh my God! Here I come, Ren & Stimpy!" Chyna rushed to put on her black leather booties.

L.A. and India didn't understand that you couldn't rush beauty. Chyna didn't go anywhere without being glam. She never knew who she might run into. Chyna threw on her army fatigue jacket and draped a black, fringe, Aldo crossbody bag over her chest. She was finally ready to go. The heels of her boots clunked as she walked down the steps.

L.A. and India were sitting on the couch waiting for her. They were both in their own world playing Candy Crush together. She loved the bond that they had created. India truly respected L.A. and always looked forward to when he came around. When he was on the road, L.A.

always checked up on her to make sure she was cool and doing well in school.

The fact that he cared about her child's well-being as well as hers caused Chyna to fall deeper in love with him. This was what she'd waited her whole entire life for. Within a blink of an eye, everything had fallen into place. She had a man that loved her, a brilliant daughter and was working for her idol. Chyna thanked God over and over for bringing L.A. into her life. Because of the unconditional love he showered her with, she'd become a better woman. She no longer wanted to play games or sleep around. Her heart belonged with him and that was where it was gonna stay.

"I'm ready."

"'Bout time," He smirked greeting her with a sensual kiss.

Chyna's knees buckled. L.A.'s kisses always had that effect on her.

"Shut up." She scrunched up her face.

"Come on." India pushed them towards the door. "You can make out later. I don't wanna miss the trailer previews."

"You bossy. I wonder where you get it from," L.A. teased.

"I'm not bossy," Chyna protested, locking the door.

"Sure, you're not, Mom," India twisted her mouth to the side.

"Y'all not gon' gang up on me." Chyna laughed as they all got into L.A.'s matte, black Mercedes Benz G Wagon.

MX Movies was less than ten minutes away so it wouldn't take them anytime to get there. They all couldn't wait to see the hit movie, Deadpool. Chyna was an avid Marvel and DC comic fan. She lost her mind every time a movie came out. The fact that it was rated R was a game changer. On the way there she had L.A. blast Rihanna's Anti album. Woo was playing. Chyna and India sang and danced in their seats. Chyna did her best impression of Rihanna and wound her hips.

"Ain't nothing else for me to talk about. Boy, show me what you wanna do." She sang to L.A. as he tried to concentrate on the road.

L.A. looked at her out of the corner of his eye. Chyna was lucky that India was in the car. If she wasn't, he would've pulled over and fucked her on the side of the road. She was looking right and smelling like a tropical rainforest. It was taking everything in him not to blow her back out. Instead, he placed his hand on her inner thigh and controlled his lustful urges.

When they got to the theater, L.A. parked the car then opened India and Chyna's doors. He wanted both of them to know that opening the door for a woman was something a man was supposed to do.

"Thank you." India said feeling like a princess.

She really liked L.A. He was always nice to her and went out of his way to make sure she was okay. India especially loved how he treated her mother. She'd never seen her mother happier. There wasn't a day that went by that she wasn't smiling. L.A. never made her cry or treated her badly like Tyreik or the white guy she dated. He treated her mom like a queen.

L.A. took Chyna's hand as they crossed the street. India closely followed by. Once they got to the entrance, he held the door open for both girls.

"Thanks, baby," Chyna's heart fluttered then dropped to her knees.

As she walked in she spotted Carlos and Bellamy coming down the staircase. Chyna and Carlos' eyes linked instantly. Chyna couldn't believe what her eyes were seeing. He had his hand wrapped around Bellamy's neck. They looked more in love than ever. He'd talked all that shit about not wanting her but there they were. *He is fuckin' pathetic,* she thought.

Chyna was so glad she was over him and all of his bull. She despised the sight of his face. It was funny how she'd gone from being head over heels in love with him to feeling like he was a joke. But none of that mattered. She was with L.A. now.

Bellamy glanced at Chyna then over at Carlos. He couldn't take his eyes off her. It was apparent that he still loved her. It was written all over his face. In order to get his attention, she palmed his jaw with her hand and made him face her. Carlos focused on her and gave Bellamy a comforting smile.

L.A. and India stepped inside the theater. Chyna stood unable to move. He wondered what had her undivided attention. Then he spotted Carlos and Bellamy. L.A. scoffed and intertwined his fingers with hers.

Carlos eyed his ex-friend and immediately put two and two together. His blood instantly began to boil. He knew that Chyna was on some fuck him type shit. He figured she'd be in her feelings for a while but eventually come back around. He never thought she'd break the code and fuck with someone he used to call friend.

What part of the game is this, he wondered as he watched L.A. take her hand. He wanted to kill them both. *How could she do this to me?* Carlos hadn't seen it coming. He thought he'd always have Chyna on his side. Had her feelings for him really gone from love to hate? He truly loved her and this was the thanks he got.

"You good?" L.A. asked Chyna.

"Yeah." She replied honestly.

For the first time in her life, she was more than good. She was great. Months before, she would've been distraught over seeing Carlos with Bellamy but not anymore. She didn't give a fuck who he spent his time with. He was free to drive another bitch crazy. If Bellamy wanted to be stuck on stupid, then that was on her. Chyna was in love. She'd completely moved on.

"Chyna?" Felicia's receptionist called her name. "Felicia wants to see you in her office."

"Okay." She stopped filing papers and went to see what Felicia wanted.

It was almost lunchtime so she probably wanted Chyna to take her lunch order. Chyna paused in front of Felicia's office door. She wasn't going to make the mistake of not being invited in first. Every time she saw Felicia, visions of her getting ate out by Warren filled her head.

Chyna wished she could remove the disturbing thought from her memory bank. Felicia still carried on like the moment never happened. Chyna found her to be a far better actress than writer. Chyna raised her hand and knocked three times.

"Come in," Felicia instructed.

Chyna opened the door and stood in front of Felicia's desk. Although she'd been working for her for quite some time she still found her to be very intimidating. Felicia was the epitome of a boss bitch. Chyna wanted badly to be in a position of power. She prayed to God that one day her hard work would pay off and she'd be a writer and show runner of her own show.

"Have a seat, please."

Chyna did as she was told. She was fully prepared to take Felicia's order.

"How have you liked working here so far?" Felicia placed her elbows on her desk and stared directly at Chyna.

"I love it. I've learned quite a lot already. Seeing the process of how the show is put together is so fascinating. I love everything about it and you have been a phenomenal mentor to me. You've taught me so much."

"I'm glad to hear that because I read your spec."

Oh, Lord, Chyna inhaled deep. *Here we go.*

"And I'm going to have to be very honest with you. It wasn't good," Felicia said bluntly.

Chyna willed herself not to breakdown and cry. She'd blew it. She'd never make it as a television writer. Her dreams were crushed. *Now what am I going to do,* she thought dying inside.

"It was great," Felicia added with a huge smile.

"Oh my God." Chyna exhaled.

She didn't even realize she'd been holding her breath the whole time.

"For a second there I thought you hated it." She placed her hand on her chest.

"You did a great job, Chyna. There were a few mistakes here and there but nothing that can't be fixed with time. So if you're tired of getting me coffee, I would like to offer you a position on the Junior Writing Team," Felicia said sincerely proud of her.

"Hell yeah, I wanna position," Chyna replied unable to contain herself.

Felicia shook her head and laughed.

"Good, it's a pleasure to have you on board." She held out her hand for a shake.

"No, thank you, Felicia." Chyna shook her hand diligently. "You're making my dreams come true. I promise, I won't let you down."

"To celebrate, I'm inviting you to Mexican night at my home tonight. The whole staff will be there."

"I will be there with bells on," Chyna said giddy, preparing to leave her office.

"Just a second," Felicia stopped her. "As your last duty as my assistant, I need you to pick up my lunch."

Several food trucks were parked outside of the office building. Felicia had a craving for 2 Girls 4 Wheels. Chyna stood in line in the damp, cold air. She was so over winter. St. Louis winters were the worse. It was always so bleak and dreary looking outside. Chyna couldn't wait for the sun to peek back out and say hello. Until spring, she'd have to settle for the cloudy sky and bone chilling winter air.

Nothing could dampen Chyna's spirits. Not even the cold weather. She'd made it! A happiness like no other filled her core. She could feel it in her veins. This was truly the American dream. She wanted to run and leap for joy. Things only got better when she received a call from L.A. She couldn't wait to tell him the good news.

"Hey, baby," she answered cheerfully. "Did your flight land already?"

"Yeah, I'm on my way to the crib now. What got you so happy?"

"I just got the best news of my life!"

"Word? Well look, I want you to tell me everything over dinner tonight."

"I'm sorry," Chyna replied sadly. "I can't. My boss is having everyone over. I can't miss it. I have to go."

"A'ight that's cool. Just hit me when you're done."
L.A. replied, disappointed that he wouldn't get to see her
face.

"I will. I can't wait to see you. When I do, I'ma give
you a big ole hug and a kiss," she promised.

"You better." L.A. said longing to see her as well.

"DON'T TAKE ADVANTAGE. DON'T LEAVE MY HEART

DAMAGED." –KHALID, "LOCATION"

CHAPTER TWENTY-ONE

Mexican night at Felicia's was not just a staff get together. It was an event. She had a world-famous chef preparing authentic Mexican dishes and two bartenders. There were sombreros, maracas, a margarita ice luge and a Mariachi band. Felicia didn't do anything half-ass. Her commitment to detail was another thing Chyna admired.

Despite her cheating on her husband, Chyna wanted to be just like her. It was nice to see her outside of the office. Felicia seemed to loosen up on her downtime. She floated around her seven-million-dollar mansion like a social butterfly. She wore a red rose in her hair and a colorful flower-printed, spaghetti-strapped dress.

Her husband, Carl, sat off to the side by himself drinking a Corona. He was a fairly nice looking older man. He was tall with honey-colored skin, hazel eyes and salt and pepper curly hair. He reminded Chyna of Rick Fox. Felicia barely paid him any attention. She'd introduced him to everyone then left him to fend for himself. Chyna felt sorry for him. After saying hello, Chyna found him to be a sweet, soft-spoken man.

As Carl sat dying for his wife's attention, a look of sadness washed over his face. Chyna wished Felicia could see how much torture he was in. She'd been in his position so she knew exactly how he felt. It was a fucked up feeling to love someone that acted like you didn't even exist. Things got even dicer when Chyna spotted Warren walk through the door. *Oh no she didn't,* she thought. *Felicia got hella balls. How she gon' invite her side nigga to her house?*

Chyna watched in shock and awe as Warren greeted her with a casual hug and a quick peck on the cheek. Felicia's whole face lit up. Chyna glanced over at Carl, who was watching their every move. *I wonder does he know.* Ready to go, Chyna finished off her drink. She had enough for the night. Seeing Felicia openly cheat on her husband was too much for even Chyna to bear.

Even she would never be that cruel. She was known to be on some ho shit but what Felicia was doing was outright wrong. She was taking things too far. Chyna had to get out of there. She felt too bad knowing the truth. Not paying attention as she rushed through the crowd to tell Felicia goodnight, Chyna ran face first into a man's broad chest.

"Shit, I'm sorry." She jerked back and looked up into the man's face.

The man was L.A.

"What are you doing here?" She asked shocked to see him there.

Did this nigga follow me here, she wondered confused.

"No. The question is what are you doing here?" He said equally perplexed.

"I told you my boss was having everyone over for dinner tonight."

"Hold up. You work for my mother?" L.A. screwed up his face.

"Your mother?" Chyna whipped her head back-and-forth like a cartoon character. "Felicia Abbot is your mom?"

"Yeah. My last name is Abbot." He tapped her on the head so she would remember.

"Oh my God. I totally forgot about that." Chyna slapped her hand against her forehead.

L.A. had only mentioned his full name to her once and that was on their first date nearly a year before. Chyna never bothered to do a full background check on him because when he first got on her she was so wrapped up in Carlos.

"So this whole time you've been working for my ole bird?"

"Yeah," Chyna replied.

"That's crazy."

"I knew she had a son but I didn't know it was you."

"I call myself stopping by to see my people in order to waste time until you got done doing what you were doing," L.A. explained.

"Wow." Chyna sighed feeling lightheaded.

Now that she knew L.A. was Felicia's son, it only further complicated things. She had to tell him what his mother was up to. She couldn't keep such a huge secret from him. She loved him too much not to tell him. It would drive her crazy if she didn't.

"There goes my baby!" Felicia held her arms open for a hug.

"Hey, Ma," L.A. hugged her.

"I thought you weren't coming." She said thrilled to see her son.

"I wasn't at first but I'm glad I did." He pulled Chyna into him.

"You know Chyna? Chyna, you know my son?" She looked back-and-forth between the two.

Unable to speak, Chyna's face turned blue/green. She felt sick.

"This is my girlfriend."

"Wow." Felicia eyed Chyna paranoid. "What a small world."

"She had no idea you were my mother," L.A. chuckled.

"Is that right?" Felicia glared at Chyna suspiciously. "Have you spoken to your father?" She changed the subject.

"No. Where is he?" L.A. looked around.

"He's around here somewhere. Go say hi. I want to speak to Chyna for a minute."

"I'll be back." He kissed Chyna on the top of her head.

"Follow me." Felicia turned her back and led Chyna to her private office.

Chyna swallowed the lump in her throat and closed the door behind her. Felicia sat on the edge of her desk and crossed her legs.

"I find it quite odd that you didn't know Lucas was my son."

"I swear to God I didn't know," Chyna swore.

"I don't know what kind of game you're playing but if you think fuckin' my son and holding my little secret over my head is gonna get you ahead, then you have another thing coming," Felicia spat with venom.

"I didn't get to where I'm at by letting conniving little bitches like you run over me."

Did she just call me a bitch, Chyna thought speechless?

"Uhhhh," Chyna chuckled appalled by Felicia's choice of words. "Felicia, I had no idea L.A. was your son and I would never try to get ahead by blackmailing you."

"Good 'cause if you want to keep your job and a good name in the industry, I would suggest you keep your mouth shut or I will be forced to bury you. Your career as a television writer will be over before it even started," Felicia threatened, uncrossing her legs. "Now, if you'll excuse me, I have a party to get back to."

Felicia knew she was going overboard with the theatrics but her career and her marriage was on the line. She liked Chyna a lot. She reminded Felicia of herself when she was younger, which is what scared her. Chyna had the "it" factor. That didn't come a dime a dozen.

She would be a show runner in no time and with the dirt she had on Felicia, her career could skyrocket even faster. Felicia couldn't leave anything to chance. She had to put the fear of God in Chyna.

"Just let me know when you're ready to roll up on the ho." Delicious plopped down on Chyna's bed.

"I can't believe she spoke to you like that," Asia joined the conversation via FaceTime.

"Me either. My idol turned into my nemesis within a matter of seconds," Chyna answered. "It was fucked up what she said to me but my feelings were more so hurt. I mean, I really look up to her. Well, I did. Y'all know how much I admired that woman. To have her think that way about me really hurts." Chyna said honestly upset.

Never in a million years did she expect to be thrown this curveball. She'd just gotten her life on track, fallen in love with the man of her dreams and been hired to work her dream job. How was she going to navigate her way out of this mess?

"I don't know what I'm going to do." She lay next to Delicious and rested her head on his shoulder.

"Keep yo' damn mouth shut!" Brooke insisted. "You just got on the writing staff. You have worked your butt off to get to this point in your career. We've been talking about this for over two years now. Now you got it. I'm not gon' let you fuck this up for us. Felicia's personal life ain't got shit to do with you. Don't tell L.A. nothin'. That's between him and his damn mama. Look at it like it's an A and B conversation and C your way out."

"You really think I shouldn't say nothin'?" Chyna asked feeling the weight of the secret on her chest.

"No!" Asia yelled through the phone. "You better tell that man the truth. He needs to know what his shady mammy is up to. If you don't tell him and he finds out that you knew, he's going to be pissed. The last thing you want him to do is start looking at you sideways. He's going to figure well, if she can keep that from me, what else could she be hiding. So to hell with what Brooke talkin' about. Don't let her get you fucked up. Tell him the truth!"

"Girl, don't listen to Carol Brady." Brooke rolled her eyes. "She don't know nothin'. You wanna keep yo' job, don't you?"

"Yeah," Chyna nodded.

"And you wanna keep your man too?"

"Of course."

"Alright then. Shut the hell up."

"I still think we need to jump the ho." Delicious smacked his lips.

He was always up to fight. Chyna sat stumped. She appreciated all of her friends' advice but didn't know which she should take. She loved L.A. She also loved the opportunity she'd been given. Hell, she hadn't even started yet. If she told L.A. about his mother's extramarital affair, she'd be giving up her dreams as a television writer for a man she hoped to spend forever with. But forever doesn't last always. Anything could happen and she and L.A. could be over within a blink of an eye. Was their budding

relationship worth risking it all?

"HE ONLY WANT ME WHEN I'M NOT THERE. HE BETTA CALL BECKY WITH THE GOOD HAIR." –BEYONCÉ, "SORRY"

CHAPTER TWENTY-TWO

Chyna and L.A. were in bed enjoying a lazy Sunday afternoon. They'd only gotten up to eat and bathe. Chyna found comfort and support in his arms. She needed his strength more than ever. She was starting her first day in The Writers' Room the following day. Her nerves were bad. She wasn't particularly thrilled about seeing Felicia. After the way she'd spoken to her, Chyna didn't want anything to do with her.

The ghetto, not-to-be-fucked-with side of her died to put Felicia in her place. She had her all the way fucked up. Instead, Chyna decided to keep her peace. She wasn't quite ready to rock the boat. The troubled waters she'd been on had just calmed down. She didn't want the craziness to come back. She'd finally found peace. No one was going to take that away from her.

Then L.A. squeezed her tight and she was reminded of the hedge of protection he poured over her. He'd done everything to prove his loyalty to her. He'd stopped with the games from the moment he stepped to her on some real shit. If she didn't tell the truth, the secret would eat her alive. All weekend she'd been a nervous wreck over it. Her stomach was in knots. She barely ate or slept.

L.A. could feel her tension. The whole weekend she'd been mentally off in her own world. He tried to act like he didn't notice it but he couldn't anymore. He needed to know what was keeping her up at night. Nervousness radiated off of her. L.A. didn't know what the problem was. He hoped she wasn't acting weird because of anything he'd done. Most of all, he hoped she wasn't changing her mind about him. Chyna was a hard girl to get close to. It took him nearly a year to get to where they were now.

She'd been so glamorized by Carlos that she couldn't see past him. L.A. had known from the minute they met that she was destined to be his. He'd be crushed if she was having second thoughts. He hoped Carlos wasn't fucking with her mind again. She said she had no communication with him. L.A. wanted to trust her word but a part of him still feared that she wasn't all the way over Carlos. L.A. stretched his long, muscular arm down her thick thigh.

"What's going through that brain of yours?" His deep, gravelly voice penetrated her ears.

Chyna rolled over onto her side to face him. Affectionately, she reached up and rubbed the side of his face. His beard tickled the palm of her hand. She could see that he was worried for her. Her uneasiness was rubbing off on him. Chyna leaned over and placed several small kisses on his chest. His light brown skin smelled like cinnamon and honey.

She never wanted to leave his side. Chyna hated that it had taken her 34 years to find him but was thankful for the life lessons that led her to him. L.A. was the one for her. He was her king, her partner in crime, her life vest, lover and friend. It was time for her to tell him what had been going on. He had to know how she'd gotten caught up in the monsoon called Felicia. *You gotta tell him,* she thought gazing into his eyes. *But I don't wanna be the one to hurt him.*

"I'm just anxious about tomorrow." She partly told the truth.

"Why? You gon' do great. My mom loves you."

If you only knew, Chyna tried her best not to roll her eyes.

"I just hope I get along with everyone and that they like me and my ideas."

"They will; you have nothing to worry about," L.A. guaranteed. "You got this."

L.A. was right. Chyna had nothing to worry about. Her first week on the Junior Writing Team went off without a hitch. Everyone liked what she brought to the table and she got along with everyone. Things between her and Felicia was awkward and strained. They both went out of their way to avoid one another. Their mentorship was officially over.

Felicia treated her like any other employee. Chyna didn't mind it much. She preferred to stay as far away from her as possible. She didn't want any parts of the mess she'd created for herself. Chyna came to work every day focused on the job at hand. She kept her head down and on the storyline for the show. It had been difficult keeping the burden of Felicia's secret on her heart but she had to keep her head above water for her and L.A.'s sake.

She didn't want to light the match that would blow his family up. She refused to destroy them. They both had to concentrate on their careers. L.A. was in the middle of basketball season. She didn't want to do anything that would upset him and take him off his game. Yeah, it was Kobe's farewell tour but L.A. still took his job very seriously.

It was the end of a long workweek. Chyna was in her favorite place: the mirror. L.A. had 24hours in town before his next game. He was dedicating all of his free time to her. That night they were going to have a romantic dinner for two at their favorite restaurant: Elaia. Elaia was located on the upper floor of a renovated house. The restaurant offered an insanely good, four-course tasting menu of Mediterranean-influenced dishes.

Chyna hadn't eaten since breakfast in preparation for the scrumptious meal. She was going to savor every morsel. It was March so the weather had warmed up a bit. Chyna was thrilled that spring was right around the corner. She couldn't take another day of winter. Ready to be on her worst behavior, she sprayed Bottega Veneta Parco Palladiano IV Eau de Parfum all over her body.

She wanted to look absolutely delectable for L.A. She hadn't had an all-white moment in ages so she decided to wear a white, spaghetti strap, bodycon dress with a thigh-high split up the side and flesh tone, strappy heels. Loving Tan Bronze Shimmer Luminous Cream shined from her neck all the way down to her toes. A gold purse in the shape of a coin finished off the simple yet highly sexy look.

Chyna felt like a bag of money as she headed towards the door. Her cab driver was outside waiting for her. Chyna told India goodbye and opened the door to find a package waiting on her doorstep. Curious as to who sent her a package, she quickly tore the packing paper off and found a scrapbook. On the cover were the words, "This Is What Happens When I Think About You".

Her heart skipped a beat. L.A. was always doing creative things to keep her on her toes. It was one of the reasons she fell in love with him. Chyna flipped the book open. Her whole face screwed up when she realized the cute little book wasn't from L.A. Carlos had sent it. On each page was a single Polaroid picture of them during their summer love affair. There were pics of them pillow fighting in bed, them sitting on the hood of his Jeep boo'd up and candid pics of her asleep in his arms.

Chyna didn't know how to feel or react to the sentimental photos. At one point she would've taken the gesture as a sign of hope but things had changed. She saw Carlos for exactly who he was. He only wanted her when he couldn't have her. It was all a game to him. Chyna had gracefully bowed out a long time ago. L.A. had her soul. He was the one who held the key to her heart in the palm of his hand.

She wanted nothing to do with Carlos. At the end of the scrapbook he wrote *can I see you*. Chyna looked down at her watch as she got in the cab. She had a half an hour until she had to be at the restaurant. Elaia was only ten minutes away. She had enough time to swing by Carlos' crib. Chyna gave the cab driver his address and sat quietly looking out of the window.

It was time to put an end to this. L.A. could've easily been at her house when the package came. If he would've been, all hell would've broken loose. Chyna didn't want Carlos calling her or sending her pictures. There would be no strolling down memory lane. She was good on him. Carlos and Chyna were finito, finished. It was high time he understood that. Chyna pulled up to his place. His car was parked outside so he was there.

She looked up at his beautiful home. A thousand emotions hit her at once. She hadn't been there in almost a year. All of the good, fun, loving moments they shared came flooding back. Conjuring up all the strength she had, Chyna told the driver she'd be right back. Chyna fixed her dress and walked up his stone steps. With the scrapbook in hand, she rang the doorbell.

Carlos came to the door drinking a glass of red wine. He wore no shirt, just a pair of Calvin Klein boxer/briefs and jeans with the knees ripped out. He was surprised to find her on his doorstep. Chyna always played hard to get. He'd sent the scrapbook hoping it would get her back. He never expected her to give in so soon.

"Hey," he spoke softly.

"Hi," Chyna replied feeling naked under his captivating gaze. "You got a minute? I need to talk to you."

"Yeah, come in." He stepped to the side.

Bellamy was on a business trip and wouldn't be home until the next day so the coast was clear. Chyna sashayed past him and walked inside. Nothing had changed. Everything was the same except the obvious feminine touches that had been added. A blind man could see that Bellamy lived there. *This nigga sending me scrapbooks and shit and he live with a whole bitch,* Chyna fumed. *Lying muthafucka.*

She was so over Carlos it wasn't even funny. Carlos closed the door behind him. Chyna looked better than ever. Li'l mama was the baddest thing around. A glow radiated off her. The white dress she wore clung to her mouthwatering breasts and curvaceous hips. He had to have her back in his life. He was over playing the back-and-forth game between her and Bellamy. Chyna was the obvious choice. She was the woman he wanted to spend the rest of his life with. He never wanted to see her with anyone but him.

Chyna placed the scrapbook down on his kitchen island and stared at him. She was determined not to get distracted by his handsome, good looks. She came to speak her peace and get the fuck up out of there.

"I see you got the book," he smiled. "You like it?"

"I came to give it back to you." Chyna slid the scrapbook across the island. "You can't be sending me stuff like that."

"Why not? You ain't like it?"

"It's not about whether I liked it or not."

"Then what is it about?" Carlos reveled in the challenge she gave him.

He missed their verbal sparring.

"I have a man," Chyna stated bluntly.

"What ya man got to do with me? I don't give a fuck about him. That shit ain't real. You and I both know it," Carlos replied, unfazed by her confession.

"I love L.A."

"That's what yo' mouth say but you and I know what it is." Carlos eased closer to her.

Chyna took two steps back.

"Fall back, bruh." She held her hand up and stopped him dead in his tracks. "Me and you are not gettin' ready to fuck."

"Who said anything about fuckin'? Unless that's really what you came here for," he smirked. "I was about to pour you a drink." He picked up the bottle of wine.

Chyna felt stupid. She'd played right into his hands. Carlos was always one step ahead of her.

"I don't want no damn wine," she spat flustered. "I came here to tell you to your face that I'm not fuckin' wit' you no more. I'm wit' L.A. now. What we had is a wrap. I'm happier than I have ever been in my life. So please respect that and leave me alone." Chyna said as gently as possible.

"You don't mean that." Carlos retorted not trying to face reality. "You need some wine. Wine always calms you down." He poured her a glass anyway.

"Are you conscious? Didn't I just tell you I don't want no fuckin' wine?!?" Chyna yelled becoming irritated.

"Chyna," Carlos held the glass of wine in his hand and stared at her. "If you don't wanna be with me, then why are you here? You could've said this shit over the phone. Face it. You still love me. You wanna be with me as much as I wanna be with you."

"You're right. I could've told you this over the phone but I wanted to look you dead in the eye when I told you to leave me the fuck alone! I don't want you! I don't want you today! I don't want you tomorrow and I for damn sure won't want you next year! There will never be a me and you! You fucked up! When you had me, you didn't want me; so deal!"

"So you just expect me to just go on like I don't love you? Like me and you never existed? I can't do that."

"You made your bed. Now lay in it. What we had will never compare to what I have with L.A. I love that man with all my heart. I would never go back to you. You ain't even half the man he is. You ain't nothing but a lying, cheating-ass, li'l boy dressed up as a man." Chyna spat maliciously.

She didn't want to take it there with him but Carlos had to see she wasn't playing. Carlos sucked his teeth and tried to maintain his cool. There wasn't a trace or a hint of a smile on her face. Chyna was dead serious. She was really over him.

"Now if you'll excuse me. I have to go. My man is waiting for me." Chyna tried to step past him but Carlos blocked her path.

When he jumped in front of her he ended up spilling the glass of wine all over her white dress. Chyna held her breath and stood frozen in time. Her dress was ruined.

"What the fuck is your problem? Look at what you've done!" She hit him on the arm so hard her hand stung.

"I'm so sorry. I didn't mean to do that," Carlos apologized.

"You fuckin' idiot!" Chyna screamed, examining the damage.

The front of her dress was covered in red wine. She couldn't go to dinner with L.A. with a huge stain on her dress. Questions of how her dress had gotten ruined would come up. Chyna didn't have any plans of telling him she'd gone to see Carlos. He'd forbad her to see him.

"I can't go to dinner like this!" She tried to wipe the stain away with a wet paper towel.

"Stop! Don't do that." Carlos took the paper towel away from her. "Take your dress off."

"I'm not taking my damn dress off!" Chyna looked at him like the idiot he was. "What the fuck is wrong with you? Are you that damn thirsty?"

"You wanna get it cleaned, don't you?"

Chyna groaned. L.A. was calling her phone. If she was going to meet him at all for dinner she had to wash the dress. Sure, she'd be hella late but she would rather be late than sorry. Over a week would pass before they got to see each other again. She had to do what she had to do. Instead of answering, Chyna sent his call to voicemail.

"Can you pay the cab driver and tell him to go ahead and leave?"

"I got you." Carlos ran outside, grinning from ear-to-ear.

His plan was working. Once the cab driver was paid and sent on his way, he walked back inside to find Chyna with her back turned. She was pulling her dress up over her head. Underneath the dress she wore nothing but a white G-string. Her caramel, shimmery-toned back and round ass was a wonderful sight to see. Carlos didn't realize until then how much he missed seeing her naked body. He couldn't pass up the opportunity to capture the moment on his camera phone.

"I TOLD YOU, BOY, THIS AIN'T WHAT YOU WANT BUT YOU DIDN'T WANNA LISTEN TO ME." — ELLE MAI, "WANTED"

CHAPTER TWENTY-THREE

Chyna was nearly an hour late when she arrived at the restaurant. L.A. was none too pleased by her tardiness. He'd taken the red-eye into town, had an intense workout, several meetings and still got there on time. When Chyna arrived frantic and flushed, he was put on guard even more. He'd called her twice and she hadn't bothered to pick up either time. He found it quite strange that she would only respond via text. She claimed to be held up at work then stuck in traffic.

L.A. wanted to believe her but Chyna's erratic behavior had him on high alert. He'd grown to know her pretty well. He knew when she was lying and she most certainly wasn't telling the truth. Something was up. He just didn't know what. Despite the weird tension between them, they were able to salvage dinner.

L.A. didn't want to ruin their night together with an argument so he put his suspicions on hold. Chyna had been nothing but a stand up woman when it came to him. He had no reason not to trust her. After dinner all he wanted was to lay her body down and make love until the sun came up. That night, he and Chyna made love underneath the strawberry moon.

A sensual hedonism took over them. All night there was a game of push and pull between them. L.A. and Chyna tried to devour one another. Into orbit they went soaring into outer space. Love making for them always transcended space and time. Everything around them went radio silent.

Moans of pleasure were the only sounds that could be heard. L.A. couldn't get enough of her. He could get lost in her honeycomb hideout forever. Each stroke felt like he was on a rocket ship being launched. Skin to skin their bodies melted and became one. L.A. kissed and licked her collarbone. With Chyna, he'd found forever. If she ever left his side he'd lose it for sure.

"L.A." Chyna whimpered on the brink of cumming.

He'd hit her with the death stroke. Chyna's lips quivered with each grind of his hips. She was addicted to his love. In between her thighs was where he belonged. The following morning, she opened her eyes and found herself in bed alone. Rubbing her eyes, Chyna rose from her slumber. Normally L.A. would still be in bed asleep.

With his hectic schedule, he liked to get as much rest as possible. Chyna flicked the covers from off her body and got out of bed. She grabbed one of L.A.'s t-shirts to put on as she went to find him. She found him sitting in the living area on the floor. The television wasn't on. He sat there staring blankly out of the bay window. A bottle of Hennessy and a glass half full sat on the coffee table before him. It was only nine o'clock in the morning. L.A. never drank that early in the day. Something was wrong.

"Love, you okay?" She sat down on the floor beside him.

Something had knocked L.A. off his square. He was distraught. Chyna hoped no one had died. *Oh my God,* she thought. *He knows about his mother.* L.A. turned and looked at her. He was so angry he couldn't even speak. If he opened his mouth and released the rage he was feeling, he was liable to kill her.

"Love." Chyna wrapped her arms around his neck. "I'm sorry. How did you find out?"

"Get off of me." L.A. pushed her away.

Chyna eyed him fearfully. She'd never seen him this angry before. His eyes were bloodshot red.

"I wanted to tell you. I just didn't know how." She tried to explain.

"You told me you were no good but I didn't believe you." L.A. finished off his drink and poured himself another. "I should've listened when you told me not to fuck with you."

"I'm so sorry." Chyna began to cry.

She knew he'd be mad when he found out about his mother's affair and the fact that she knew. She never envisioned it being this bad. *You should've told him, you idiot.*

"I swear to God I wanted to tell you. I just didn't think you should find out from me."

"You would've rather I find out that you were still fuckin' Carlos via Instagram?" He shoved his phone in her face.

Chyna reared her head back and focused her attention on the picture he was showing her. Carlos had posted a picture of her with her back facing the camera as she took off her dress. Her entire back and ass was out. The caption said: I knew I'd get her back in my bed. All of the air inside Chyna's lungs turned to ice. When she woke up that morning she never thought that her world would be crashing down around her.

"Love, it's not what you think," she panicked.

"It all makes sense now. That's why you were late for dinner and acting all strange 'cause you were with him." L.A. put it all together. "That's why you weren't answering your phone."

"It's not what it looks like though. I went over there to tell him to leave me alone. I told him I love you." Chyna cried so hard her chest hurt.

"You told him you love me before or after you took off your dress and fucked him?" L.A. said mockingly.

"Noooo... you have it all wrong. He spilled wine on my dress and I was taking it off to wash it."

"Yeah a'ight, Chyna. You gon' sit here and lie to my face? I ain't been nothing but good to you and this is how you do me? I've been nothin' but straight up with you."

"I love you! I would never cheat on you," she replied truthfully.

"Then what were you doing with him?!" L.A. barked.

"He sent me this lame-ass scrapbook filled with pictures of us and at the end of the book he wrote a li'l note asking could he see me. Only reason I went over there is to give him the book back and tell him to his face that I was good. Baby, I love you." Chyna tried to palm L.A.'s face with her hands only to be pushed away again.

"You have to believe me. I swear to God. I'm tellin' you the truth," she pleaded.

L.A. rose to his feet to get away from her. He could see the desperation on her face. She was willing to do everything in her power to get him to believe her. The proof was in the pudding. There was no way he could. Chyna was a liar and a manipulator disguised as an angel.

"I ain't gotta believe shit. The picture says everything! You got this muthafucka out here making me and you look stupid. This shit is all over the internet! People all under my comments and shit talkin' about your girl is a ho, dawg. You don't deserve that. Like I'ma l'il bitch! My teammates have seen this shit! You know how fucked up this is? How could you do this to me?" He threw the bottle of Hennessey against the wall.

Glass shattered and fell to the floor. Splatters of liquor stained the wall.

"I put nothin' before you! I put my all into this. I loved you and your daughter and this is how you do me?" A tear slipped from L.A.'s eye.

"I'm sorry." Chyna wept inside her hands.

There was no way she could fix this besides going back in time. L.A. hated her. She could feel him slipping further and further away. This wasn't going to end with him accepting her apology and them moving on. There would be no fairytale ending.

"I asked you were you over him and you said yeah."

"I am! I swear!" Her heart broke into a million pieces. "I don't fuck with that man. All I want is you." Tears streamed from her eyes.

"Save it. You need to be happy a nigga like me even noticed you. You know how many chicks I passed up to be with you?"

"L.A., you gotta believe me. I'm telling you the truth."

"Just get your shit and get the fuck out." He said done with the conversation.

He wasn't about to let her see him get emotional.

"L.A., please," Chyna begged.

"Shuuuut up!" He waved her off. "Just go!"

He couldn't stomach the sight of her anymore. He would rather be by himself. There was no need to argue and fight. Chyna had hurt him to the core. He'd never be able to get over what she'd done. Things would never be the same. He now saw her as the devil. And to think, he was just about to give her an engagement ring.

Chyna didn't want to leave but she had no choice. They were anything but themselves at that point. Continuing to plead her case was futile. He'd never believe that she was telling the truth. The picture made her look guilty. Maybe in some weird way she was.

She'd fumbled his heart. She should've stayed away from Carlos. Once again, she'd fallen into his trap. Maybe Chyna wasn't worthy of love. She always found a way to fuck it up. Her past always seemed to mess up her future. Maybe she'd done too much dirt, fucked too many men, played too many games, told too many lies. Maybe she got in her own way. All Chyna knew for sure was that the man she shared a love so special and rare with was no longer hers. L.A. breaking up with her was the worst pain she ever felt.

Enraged, Chyna left L. A's house and headed straight to Carlos' place. She had to know why he'd done it. Chyna raced up the steps and banged on the door. Carlos groggily came to the door. He was still in bed asleep. Chyna found it amusing that he could sleep through the chaos he'd created. Chyna didn't even bother saying a word. She reared her hand back and slapped him so hard his lip began to bleed. Not done, she continued to slap him until he found a way to restrain her.

"Why did you do it? Huh? Why did you do it? What have I ever done to you to make you do something like that to me?" She screamed so loud the neighbors could hear.

"You chose him!" Carlos shouted back, squeezing her arms.

His veins were popping out of his neck. After seeing her at the movies with L.A., something went off inside of him. It was like he was back in school. He'd become invisible all over again. Chyna acted like he didn't exist. She only had eyes for L.A. She knew how Carlos felt about him. She knew all about the rivalry. There was no way he was going to let L.A. win.

They'd been on an even playing field for years. L.A. got into the NBA and Carlos married their high school homecoming queen. If L.A. got Chyna that would put him over the top. She was the ultimate prize. Carlos put his heart on the line when he sent her the scrapbook. He was ready to let Bellamy and their past go. Chyna was finally going to get what she'd always wanted... him.

How dare she not want him now that he wanted her? She was supposed to be happy. Instead, she spit in his face and turned him away. Carlos always got what he wanted. He hated to lose; especially when it came to L.A. If Chyna didn't want him, he was going to make sure L.A. didn't want her either. Carlos wasn't going to be the only one left out in the cold. If he was going to risk it all and lose, then everybody else would too.

"This is all a game to you?" Chyna eyed him with disgust.

"What can I say? I hate to lose," Carlos said smugly.

"You lost me a long time ago," Chyna confirmed, snatching her arms away. "Did you even think about my daughter when you posted that bullshit?"

Carlos stood silent. He'd completely forgotten about India and how it would affect her.

"She's gonna see this shit! If she hasn't already! The kids at her school are gonna see it and probably make fun of her! You completely humiliated me and for what? 'Cause I didn't want your tired, pale ass? Is this some white privilege shit you on? L.A. thinks I slept wit' you! You and I both know that ain't true! I don't want nothin' to do with you!"

"That's fine." Carlos shrugged his shoulders.

He didn't care. He'd be okay. He still had Bellamy to fall back on.

"After today, stay the fuck out of my life or I swear to God I'ma kill yo' ass!" Chyna mushed him in the forehead then turned to walk away.

When she spun around, she was surprised to see Bellamy standing at the bottom of the steps with a suitcase resting at her feet. She'd returned from her trip and overheard the entire conversation. The entire flight home her insides felt like they were going to fall out of her ass. Carlos had done the unthinkable.

Bellamy was staggered when she saw his IG post. She didn't know what had gotten into him. The man was off his rocker. His obsession with being on top was ruining him. He was obviously on some fuck the world type shit. He'd set Chyna up just to spite L.A. Things had officially gotten out of hand. Chyna stomped down the steps.

"You wanted him so bad. You can have him. He's all yours, girl." She shot in Bellamy's ear on her way over to her cab.

Bellamy didn't even bother saying anything back. Her beef wasn't with Chyna. It was with Carlos. He'd humiliated her for the last time. It would be a cold day in hell before she ever let him do it again. Giving him a look that could kill, Bellamy picked up her suitcase and started walking down the street. There was no way in hell she was stepping foot back into that house.

"Where you going?" Carlos jogged down the steps.

Bellamy kept walking and pretended like she didn't even hear him. There was nothing left to say. Carlos had dug his own grave.

"Oh, so it's like that? You call yo'self being mad too? It's cool; you'll be back! Both of y'all will be back!" He yelled, trying to believe his own hype.

Deep down inside, Carlos knew the truth. His desire to win and one-up L.A. had completely backfired. He'd had two great women that loved and adored him. He'd chosen to play with their hearts. Now instead of having either of them, he was left alone. He'd lost both.

"WHEN THE FLOOR IS MORE FAMILIAR THAN THE CEILING." –

EMELI SANDÉ, "BREAKING THE LAW"

CHAPTER TWENTY-FOUR

By the time Chyna returned home, she was emotionally and physically drained. Her phone hadn't stopped ringing. All of her friends and family were blowing her up. Chyna knew that they were concerned about her well-being but she didn't have the strength to talk to anyone. She wanted to curl up in bed and hide underneath the covers. Her life was ruined.

Everyone on the blogs was calling her a ruthless, scandalous, cheating-ass bitch. Everyone was telling L.A. to dump her. Chyna wanted to lay down and die. She didn't know how she'd ever be able to go on living. She was a laughing stock. Distraught, she walked into the house like a zombie.

She felt feeble and weak. It was as if a part of her had died. L.A. was the love of her life and now he was gone. Chyna kicked off her heels and sighed. She was home. Home was her safe haven. She didn't have to answer anyone's questions. She didn't have to prove herself there.

She wouldn't be made fun of. She'd be safe behind the confines of her home.

India stepped out into the hallway and glared at her mother. Chyna looked back at her with sorrow and regret. She could tell by the look on her face that India was well aware of what was going on. India always looked at her like she was the greatest thing on earth. Now she looked at her with nothing but contempt. *Not her too,* Chyna thought. She couldn't take her baby looking at her like she was Satan. India was the only thing she had left.

"Indy, let me explain—"

"No! You ruin everything." India rolled her eyes at her mom then slammed the door so hard the walls shook.

When Monday morning rolled around, Chyna didn't want to get out of bed. She found solace hiding from the world. All she'd done was cry and ask God why. The whole world hated her. Once the memes started, she had to delete all of her social media accounts. She didn't need that kind of stress and bullying in her life. It was bad enough that neither L.A. or India was speaking to her. They both were giving her the silent treatment.

It sucked the way they were treating her. She hadn't even done anything wrong. She wished that they would believe her. The truth wasn't on her side. The perception that she'd slept with Carlos was all people cared about. Nobody wanted to know the truth. She had no way of vindicating herself. All she could do was ride things out until the scandal blew over.

Chyna went to work with black, Chanel, bug-eyed shades covering her eyes. Her eyes were damn near swollen shut from crying all weekend. As soon as she walked into the office, all eyes were on her. All of the writers started to whisper, point and shake their heads. Chyna wanted to run back home and hide underneath her bed but she had a job to do.

She wasn't going to let all of the negative press run her off her job. She wasn't going to let Carlos have that kind of power over her life. Chyna didn't even get to put her purse down on her desk before she was called into

Felicia's office. Chyna knocked on the door then went in and sat down.

"This won't take long so you can stand," Felicia instructed, concentrating on the script before her.

Chyna exhaled slowly and stood up. She was not in the mood for Felicia's shit. After making her wait a little bit, Felicia finally took her eyes off the script. A pair of red-rimmed reading glasses sat on the bridge of her nose.

"In light of your recent scandal, I have no choice but to let you go. I can't have that kind of negative press tied to my show. You can disgrace yourself but you won't take my show or my son down with you."

Chyna swallowed hard and nodded her head. She was sick of everyone running over her and talking to her crazy.

"I've tried to hold my tongue with you but you have a lot of nerve, bitch."

"Excuse you." Felicia removed her glasses and rolled her neck.

"You heard me. I'm not like you. I don't go around cheating. I would never do anything to hurt your son. I love L.A.; so before you try to crucify me and hang me on the cross, take a look in the mirror, homegirl. Get your extramarital affairs in order."

"How dare you speak to me like that? Get out of here. You're fired!"

"You said that already." Chyna rolled her eyes, ready to leave. "And by the way, you really need to stop cheating on your husband. You're too damn old for that shit. Passing around that vintage vagina will get you nowhere. Trust me, I know. Carl is a good man. He deserves so much more from you and so does L.A." She threw her building pass down onto Felicia's desk.

Chyna didn't want to be anywhere she wasn't welcome. Her pride and dignity was far more precious to her than a writing job. She valued herself way too much to let anyone treat her like shit. Fuck Felicia Abbot!

For days Chyna had been unable to move. Her limbs couldn't bend to sit or walk. Chyna could only lay flat on her stomach, face down on the pillow and cry. Her heart had been ripped out of her chest. Everyone was against her. She was the most hated woman in America. Chyna couldn't take all of the negativity. She'd gained the world to lose it all. Her life had gone from magic to shit.

Unable to cope, she isolated herself. She didn't want to face the harsh reality of what was being said about her. To have the whole word against you was one hell of a thing. What made matters worse was that L.A. wouldn't talk to her. She'd called him so much her fingers nearly started to bleed. Instead of sending her to voicemail or blocking her calls, he simply let the phone ring.

The punishment was far worse than anything Chyna could mentally or physically handle. It nearly killed her when she learned he'd been communicating with India and not her. He'd called her a few times to check and make sure she was ok. He stressed to India that if she needed anything not to hesitate to call.

The fact that he cared enough about her daughter to see about her well-being made Chyna fall in love with him even more. He truly cared about India. L.A. was the sweetest man she'd ever known. Chyna questioned India if he'd asked about her but L.A. didn't want anything to do with her. Chyna was devastated.

She needed a miracle. She needed a resurrection. The only problem was, she just didn't know how to dig herself out of the hole she'd created. All she had left was herself and God. She prayed to him every day for guidance and help. God had brought her through far worse things so she was sure he would pick her up and lead her down the right path. Until the sky cleared, she was content with sleeping her way through the insanity.

"Uh ah, girl! Get up!" Brooke flicked on the light switch.

Chyna sighed heavily. She hadn't called Brooke over and frankly didn't want any company. She liked being miserable. It was kind of fun to her.

"Brooke, turn off my damn light." Chyna pulled the covers up over her head.

"I will not." Brooke put down her purse. "I refuse to let you spend one more minute in this bed."

"Yeah, girl, 'cause it's smelling a li'l ripe up in here." Delicious held his nose. "When the last time you washed yo' ass?"

"Somebody pass me the Febreze." Asia tried to hold her breath.

She'd flown all the way in from Chicago to check on her friend. When one of the girls was down, the others stopped everything to be there for them. It was how they rolled. They were sisters.

"Asia, is that you?" Chyna hid her face.

"Yes, honey, and you stink." She sprayed the whole room then sat beside her on the bed.

"What are you doing here?"

"I came to see you, poo-poo. Question." Asia peeked underneath the covers. "Have you brushed your teeth today?"

"No."

"You ain't lying about that." Asia tooted her mouth up to her nose.

She quickly pulled the covers back over Chyna's head.

"Look, sweetie, I know when you get sad you go through this little no eating, no sleeping, no television, no bathing, no going anywhere thing but can we please take not bathing off the list? It's so unattractive."

"Let's not forget unhygienic," Delicious added.

"Yassssss, you gotta keep it cute, honey," Asia advised.

"It smell like Rick Ross left titty up in here." Delicious bugged up.

"Y'all don't understand. I'm hurting right now. I'm depressed."

"Girl, your heart is hurting; that ain't got shit to do with you washing yo' ass," Brooke quipped.

"Here." She threw a set of pajamas, a pair of panties and a towel onto her bed. "Get yo' ass up and wash in between yo' legs!"

"Come on, sweetie. You gotta get up." Asia slowly peeled the covers back.

She didn't want to release the funk too fast.

"I don't want to," Chyna whined. "Go home! Y'all gettin' on my nerves."

"Don't nobody care!" Brooke shot back. "We came over here to help you out. You can't get that man back with a fishy ass. It smells like a whole Asian fish market up in here."

Chyna tried to be mad but couldn't help cracking up laughing. She hadn't laughed in days. The feeling was phenomenal. Laughter was exactly what she needed. It was the best remedy for her sadness.

"I ain't got no fishy ass, bitch!" Chyna threw a pillow at her head.

"You do right now." Delicious pretended to gag.

"Stop exaggerating. I don't smell that bed." Chyna smelled underneath her arm. "Ooh." She winced.

"And you thought we was lying. Smell like a whole Chipotle up under there, don't it?" Delicious joned.

"What I'ma do, y'all? India nor L.A. will forgive me." Chyna fell back onto the bed. "I can't take them being mad at me anymore."

"That's why we're here. We're your fairy godmothers," Asia gleamed, running her fingers through Chyna's curly hair. "We talked to Indy. We explained to her that you didn't do anything wrong—"

"Lies you tell," Brooke cut her off. "She did do something wrong. She shouldn't have taken her dumb-ass over to his house."

"Brooklyn!" Asia gasped.

"Don't Brooklyn me. Y'all know damn well I'm tellin' the truth. Y'all just too chicken shit to say it. If she wouldn't have ever went over there, she wouldn't be in this predicament now. I'm sorry, friend, but you brought all of this on yourself."

"I thought I was doing the right thing." Chyna poked out her bottom lip.

"You thought wrong." Brooke chuckled. "What would possess yo' dumb-ass to strip down naked in front of him? You know white men are the devil."

"I was trying to get my dress clean. All I was thinking about was getting to L.A."

"Well, you fucked up, friend."

"Whatever, Towanda." Chyna compared Brooke to Tamar Braxton's hating-ass sister.

"Don't get mad at me 'cause I'm tellin' the truth. Didn't nobody tell you to try to be Captain America and try and save the day. You should've paid Carlos dust when he sent you that raggedy-ass notebook."

"It was a scrapbook," Chyna corrected her.

"Whatever. It was some bullshit," Brooke rolled her eyes.

"I bet you gon' leave that white meat alone now, ain't you?" Delicious teased.

"It ain't got nothing to do with him being white. She just fell in love with the wrong man." Asia stuck up for her friend.

"I just want my man back!" Chyna wailed, exasperated.

"Well, we can't help you get L.A. back. You gon' have to do that on your own. What we can do is get things back on track with your child. India! Bring yo' li'l bad-ass here!" Brooke shouted.

"My baby ain't bad. She's perfect." Chyna checked her as India came up the steps.

Chyna looked at her daughter and smiled. She was such a beautiful young lady. Her pretty, curly hair framed her heart-shaped face.

"Hey, Ma," India spoke shyly.

"Hi, baby."

"I'm sorry for being mad at you. I should've listened to you when you tried to tell me the truth."

"It's ok. You had every right to feel the way you did. Mama fucked up."

"I'm not gonna use the F word," India giggled. "You were trying to do the right thing and sometimes doing the right thing will still get you in trouble."

"When did you get so smart?" Chyna said proud of her daughter for being so wise.

"You taught me everything I know," India blushed.

"Come here. Give me a hug." Chyna held her arms wide-open.

"Uh ah, girl!" Asia, Brooke and Delicious jumped back. "Don't do that! You tryin' to kill us?"

"Yeah, Ma, can we not hug?" India grimaced. "I don't want your funk to rub off on me."

"IF MY HEART'S WHAT YOU WANTED, YOU CAN HAVE IT. RIP IT RIGHT OFF MY SLEEVE." -STACY BARTHE, "WAR IV LOVE"

CHAPTER TWENTY-FIVE

Spring was in full affect. The sun was shining, birds were chirping, the leaves had turned green. A month had passed since the scandal. It didn't take long for people to gravitate to the next salacious story. Chyna was happy that the heat was off of her. She was finally able to rejoin society without being mocked. She and India were bosom buddies again.

India was the one to keep her sane during the long, lonely nights. She encouraged her mother to dust herself off and act like the boss bitch she was. During her month-long hiatus, Chyna concentrated on her career. She got quiet and got focused. Whenever things went bad in her life, she started to write.

Submerging herself in her work always helped center her. She could leave her troubles behind and live the lives of her characters. Chyna got in the zone and wrote the third installment to her book series based on her life. The third book was titled Heartless. She poured her heart and soul into the novel. When it was released, her readers reveled over her sexualized tale of finding love again only to be left in the cold.

Chyna was able to tell the story so well because all of her life she'd dealt with pain. She'd been betrayed so many times it was no longer new to her. It was strange for anyone, especially a man, to treat her right. Meeting a man like L.A. - with his stature, good looks and manners - was foreign to her. She thought men like him only existed in the books she wrote.

He was the embodiment of what a real man was supposed to be. He was an African king. He was her man. She loved him immensely. Each day they spent apart was like dying a slow death but Chyna dealt with the pain and never gave up. Not a day went by where she didn't reach out to him via text or a call. She was determined to get him back. Now that she'd had a taste of him she could never let him go. With the success of Heartless, Chyna could see the grey skies clearing but things would never be the same until L.A. was back by her side.

No one was as surprised as Chyna when she received an invitation in the mail from Felicia to attend The Girlfriend Experience season 3 premiere party. She thought it was a joke until she called the office for confirmation. Her name was on the guest list. It hadn't been an error. Felicia had personally invited her there. Chyna wasn't sure if she should go. She didn't want any trouble. She had contributed a ton of ideas during her short stint on the Junior Writing Team. It would be nice to see her work play out on screen. She'd dreamt of the moment since she decided she wanted to work in television.

After a week of debating, she decided to put on her big girl panties and go. Plus, she hoped that if she went there might be a chance she'd run into L.A. If she saw him face-to-face and he saw the sincerity in her eyes, maybe he'd take her back. On the day of the party, Chyna put on her Sunday's best. Nothing expressed her emotions more than black leather.

Chyna walked onto the red carpet with a black leather jacket draped over her shoulders. A black leather, Dolce & Gabbana, spaghetti-strapped, bustier dress with a thigh-high zipper slit kissed her skin. A brand new, sickening pair of black Louboutin Pigalle heels accentuated her silky, smooth legs. A bold red lip vibrated from her full lips. She looked like a badass. She felt like one. Chyna had gotten her power back. She was back in control.

The only other time Chyna had ever been on the red carpet was when she interviewed celebrities at the 2013 MTV Movie Awards for Perez Hilton. It was a glorious feeling to be on the other side of the velvet rope. Chyna walked the red carpet with her shoulders back and her head held high. Bright lights from the cameras flashed before her face. The photographers screamed and shouted her name. This was where she belonged.

I could get used to this, she beamed. Chyna posed and smiled like a pro. She'd been preparing her whole life for this moment. Her grandmother, Pat, was surely smiling down on her from heaven. After working the red carpet, Chyna ducked inside the theater without doing any press. Some of the reporters recognized her face. She could see the hungry look in their eyes. They wanted a juicy story and rehashing the Instagram scandal would make for a great headline. Chyna wasn't going to feed the hungry wolves.

She was there to see the premiere episode, prayerfully talk to L.A. and leave with him. The season premiere was mind-blowing. All of Chyna's ideas made it onto the screen. She'd never been more proud of herself. She'd made it! Once the premiere ended, she searched the whole venue for L.A. but didn't find him anywhere.

Disappointed, Chyna hit her girls up so they could meet her for drinks. She had to celebrate her success. Before she made it out of the party she was stopped by Felicia. Chyna drunk in her look. Despite her being a bitter, evil bitch, Felicia looked like a million bucks. A head full of waterfall curls floated past her shoulders. She wore a chic, red dress that stopped right above her knees and gold heels.

"Can I talk to you for a second?" She asked.

Chyna eyed her for a second before responding. The last time she saw Felicia things got pretty heated. Chyna was not in the mood for round two.

"Yeah, sure." She said reluctantly.

Due to the fact that it was loud inside of the theater, Felicia escorted her outside. The sun was beginning to set.

"Have a seat." Felicia sat down on a bench.

Chyna sat beside her and crossed her legs.

"I want to apologize to you."

Is she talking to me, Chyna looked around, confused.

"You talkin' to me?" She pointed to her chest.

"Yes, I'm talking to you," Felicia laughed. "I was a total bitch to you. I took all of my fears of being exposed out on you and you didn't deserve that. You were 100% right. I wasn't living right. I wasn't being a good wife. Instead of dealing with the problems that my husband and I had, I sought comfort from another man," she confessed.

"I had no business treating you the way I did. I allowed my personal life to overcloud my judgment and my business. You were my employee. A damn good one at that. I should've separated the two. I didn't and I will forever be sorry for that."

Chyna was dumbfounded. She never thought that she would get an apology from Felicia. That wasn't how she saw their little pow wow going at all.

"Thanks for the apology." Chyna said truly grateful.

"No, thank you. The work you did on the show was really good. I see you having a really successful career in television writing, Chyna. You have that 'it' factor that most writers don't have. You connect with your audience in a way that most writers can't. You're real, raw and honest. Never lose that."

"I won't." Chyna took in all of the compliments Felicia was giving.

"If you'd like your old job back, I'd love to have you." Felicia held her hand.

"Hell yeah, I want my job back!" Chyna shrilled unable to control herself.

Felicia hung her head and chuckled a bit.

"You know, you really learn a lot about a person's character after you've done them wrong. I was shocked when after the way I treated you that you didn't go and tell my son all the dirt you had on me."

"I was never going to say anything. It wasn't my place," Chyna replied.

"Thank you for that. I'm glad you didn't because it was up to me to tell Lucas and my husband the truth about what I'd done. Which I did. My son is very upset with me right now. I don't blame him. I deserve everything I'm getting."

"Wow. How are things between you and your husband?"

"We're in couple's therapy. I'm determined to save my marriage."

"That's good. I hope you all are able to work things out," Chyna said sincerely. "How is—"

"L.A." Felicia answered for her.

"Yes, how is he doing?" Chyna died to know.

"Despite having to deal with my nonsense, he's okay. He's taking everything one day at a time."

"I'm happy to hear that." Tears welled in Chyna's eyes.

"You miss him, don't you?"

"Everyday." Chyna answered truthfully. "I know it looks crazy but I'm tellin' the truth, Felicia. I never slept with Carlos. He set me up."

"It does look strange." Felicia put it out there. "But I believe you."

"Thank God!" Chyna hung her head back, elated. "What can I do to get L.A. to see that I'm tellin' the truth?"

"You have to give him time."

Chyna nodded her head. Felicia was right. Time was the only thing on her side and her best option.

"After everything I've done to my husband, he hasn't given up on me. Don't give up on my son." Felicia squeezed her hand then stood up. "Now if you'll excuse me, I have a party to attend."

"Thank you for the apology and believing me, Felicia."

"Thank you for loving my son." Felicia winked her eye and headed back inside.

All alone, Chyna sat absorbing the cool, night air. Pink and orange hues cascaded over the sky. She didn't care if it took her a month, a year or an eternity. She wasn't going to give up until she was back in L.A.'s arms. Loving him was too amazing to ever let go. He was the person God put her on earth to be with. He was her paradise. L.A. could have whatever he wanted. If he wanted her to rip her heart out of her chest and hand it to him on a silver platter, she would.

And yes, at the moment he wasn't fucking with her. It hurt like hell to have him hating her but she planned on spending the rest of her life with him. Chyna was willing to do whatever she had to do to make things right. Not having him as her man wasn't an option. He was hers and that was never going to change. Chyna pulled out her phone. She had to let him know how she felt. It didn't matter if he didn't respond. She had to get her feelings off her chest.

<Messages   L.A.   Details

I love u with all my heart. I know things look really crazy but u have to believe me, L.A. I would never cheat on u. Never. And I don't care if it takes me a lifetime to get u back. I'ma wait on u.

THE END... FOR NOW

Made in the USA
Las Vegas, NV
11 December 2024

13823016R00203